'TiL DEATH

To Julie,
The brave adventurer who found
riches untold in the Tomb of Terror!

— *[signature]*

'til Death

ISBN-10: 0-9965559-1-9
ISBN-13: 978-0-9965559-1-3

First Printing

Edited by Bluebird Editing
Cover by M.S. Corley

For more information:

Website: jasonanspach.com
Facebook: facebook.com/authorjasonanspach
Twitter: @Jonspach

My newsletter pals receive updates, free books, exclusive sneak-peaks and more!
Sign up today:
bit.ly/anspach-news

For Jenn,

The love of my life and a wife worth Returning for.

CHAPTER ONE

Wednesday was pot roast night.

Alice Rockwell stared at the frozen slab of beef in her kitchen sink. If she turned up the oven temperature, perhaps Frank would have a dinner that was only half frozen... once he made it through the charcoal exterior, that is. Her husband would be upset about not having pot roast, but he'd be downright disconsolate with no dinner at all.

Resting her elbows on the gold-speckled Formica counter, Alice pondered suitable alternatives. She could still serve the potatoes and green beans she canned last summer. And if she fried tomorrow's pork chops tonight, Frank would be satiated at the very least.

The pot roast would have to wait until Thursday.

Resolute, she straightened herself and smoothed back a few stray strands of her auburn hair, which was only now showing the first meager streaks of gray. Frank had been completely gray by forty. She turned, swift enough for her mint green house dress to whisper a zipping sound against her nylons as it whirled around her legs. With heels clicking across the checkerboard floor, Alice began to cook.

At five minutes to seven Alice had pearls on, hair dressed, red lipstick freshly applied, and the dining room table set elegantly for two. Her husband was far less likely to fuss whenever Alice was "dolled up." She stood with her hands clasped in front of her, waiting for her husband to enter the front door.

Frank was a creature of habit, she knew. He would leave his office at Rockwell Fiduciary at five. His Wednesday bowling league began at five-thirty. From there he would come home and eat his supper at seven. Alice often joked with her friends that she could set the clocks by Frank's routine.

With Frank not yet home, she began to run through her explanation of how things went off the rails today. She hadn't changed the sheets or cleaned the windows yesterday because of her headache, so there was already extra work. Then Collette Peterson came by to solve some accounting problem the Ladies Missionary Society was experiencing, and everyone knows just how long Collette Peterson can talk. Then Mrs. Ernst from next door called to see if Alice would walk her to the grocery store, her speed matching her aging body. And, before she knew it the dinner hour was upon her and the pot roast was still frozen in the sink. Yes, that pretty much summed up her day. All she would need to add was, "Please forgive me, dear," and Frank's temper should be kept relatively at ease. Maybe she'd get off with just a lecture on the importance of unwavering self-discipline for success in life.

Her explanation committed to memory, Alice was startled to see that it was ten minutes past seven. Had the bowling game gone longer than expected? She sat down and began thumbing through the pages of her latest copy of Look. Another ten minutes passed, her stomach growling incessantly. Rubbing one arm, she rose and went into the kitchen. She dialed for her husband's office, thinking he may have forgotten something on his way out. Frank was punctual when it came to his desires, but was less than considerate about her time.

Alice did not hear Frank enter the house as the phone rang unanswered in her ear. Dropping the receiver, she unleashed a surprised yip when his voice cannonballed into the kitchen from the living room.

"Alice!" he shouted.

"Coming, dear." She hung up the phone, exiting the kitchen to greet her husband.

"Ho ho! Day of days, Alice!"

"I'm sorry, Frank. My day has been difficult, too. You see first Collette came by and—"

"A trifle!" interrupted the belligerent. "Not even pot roast is going to save this day! Unbelievable!"

Alice entered the dining room and saw her husband standing with his coat draped over his arm, his hat still resting on his head.

"Take your hat off, Frank. Now about the pot roast..."

Frank pulled his hat tightly to his head, slightly twisting

it in defiance. He saw on the table an alien supper seeking his approval from white china. With hands rooted to his hips, he lifted a desolate face to Alice.

"No pot roast?" he whimpered.

"I'm sorry, it's just that Collete Peterson—"

"No pot roast, even!" he exploded. "A man like me never catches a break, I tell you. The nerve of some people!"

"You're being unreasonable, dear. We can have pot roast tomorrow night."

"Not you. Them... or him— however many it was! And on bowling and pot roast night!" Frank circled a finger in the air for emphasis, "That's what really steams me!"

"You're not making any sense. What happened, dear?" Alice asked, crossing the room towards her gesticulating husband.

"What happened?!" Frank echoed, his face red from the effort. "The worst day of my life, that's what happened."

"Oh, darling." Alice closed the gap between herself and her husband and felt a matrimonial pull to rest her hand and head on Frank's chest, something that always seemed to sooth him. Her eyes enlarged in surprise as her hand passed through his body like a wind through fog.

"Fraaank!" Alice yelped with a backwards jerk, hastily removing her hand from the chill miasma. "Did you die today?"

"It is," Frank said, removing his hat to bring it slowly to his bosom, "as you say." In reverence for his now past life, he screwed his head slightly up and to his right, staring into the heavens.

Alice took another step back as Frank held his pose. It was an exact imitation of a statue he once saw of Admiral Porter. Frank felt resplendent with somber and regal airs. He waited for the sobbing to begin.

"You look ridiculous," Alice said dismissively.

Frank threw his hat to the ground where it passed silently through the oak floor. "I do not!" he spat. "I'm the very picture of dignity."

Alice rolled her eyes.

"My death deserves a certain level of decorum, Alice!"

"I'm sorry, dear. This is all so sudden. I hadn't expected this for another, well, five years or so."

"I'm only fifty-one and in my prime!" Frank shouted. "I had plenty more than five years left. My great-grandfather Sherman lived to eighty-nine!"

Alice sat down at the table and took her utensils. Frank wrinkled his nose and curled his lip at her. "See how yonder widow grieves," he said lithely.

"We widows in the land of the living must take care not to starve, lest we join our husbands too soon. Can you sit?"

"I haven't fallen through the floor, have I?"

Frank walked to the dining room table and grabbed the back of his upholstered seat only to watch his hands pass through, fingers wiggling on the other side. Alice looked from the corner of her eyes as he tried twice more with similar results.

"I think I'll stand," Frank said.

Alice nodded and took a bite of cold beans. "Did you just die, Frank? Heart attack? Hit by a bus on the walk home?"

"No." He watched her take another bite of beans. "It was a few hours ago. I was still in my office. I heard a boom, felt a sharp pain in my back and then, WHAM-O! I was in that marble hall the Returns always mention."

Alice raised her eyebrows, chewing thoughtfully. "I didn't figure you to go straight up there. You haven't been to church three times in the last two years."

"That Pastor of yours," Frank barked, jabbing his finger towards Alice, "would have me believe that a man who enjoys a nice cigar or glass of rye is a Judas!"

"Well, I'm glad you didn't go straight down either, dear."

"Thank you." Frank nodded as he rubbed the front of his still-starched shirt.

Picking up her plate, Alice walked to the kitchen sink. Frank remained in the dining room, pacing back and forth. "Why did they send you back?" Alice called over the noise of the faucet.

"Oh." Frank shrugged. "They didn't say."

"They didn't say?" Alice was piqued. She turned the water off and walked back to the dining room. "But they always say!"

"Not a peep." Frank lowered himself into the seat Alice left open. He gave each leg a double glance, clapped his hands and let out a triumphal whoop of accomplishment. He'd get the hang of being incorporeal.

"Frank!" Alice's forehead wrinkled as her still-wet hands rested on her hips. "Now I am worried. You die today of a 'sharp pain' in the back, you're made a Return without being told why, and now what? How are you supposed to move on?"

Frank held his hand out plaintively as Alice folded her arms. An alarming sense that her husband was content to take this life of the in-between as an early retirement was growing in her. Everyone died, yes. And occasionally they would come back to help clear up some unfinished problem deemed too important to let go. But they never just stuck around.

A savage rapping on the front door jolted Alice from her reflections.

"Now who could that be? It's dinner time, after all." Frank frowned towards the front door.

Two more cadences of loud and rapid knocking sounded as Alice approached the door. She opened it, flinching at the fist held at eye level, ready to hammer on the door again.

A police officer quickly lowered his arm and blushed at Alice's surprise. "My apologies Mrs..." his sentence trailed off and became a question.

"I'm Alice Rockwell."

"Mrs. Rockwell. Thank you. I'm Officer Dalton. May I come inside?" The officer rubbed his chin with the tips of his fingers. "I have some news that I'm afraid will be difficult for you to hear."

"Please, come in." Alice glanced quickly toward Frank and stepped back to allow the officer entry. "Is it about my husband?"

Dalton took a few steps inside, removed his cap, and appraised the home from the foyer. These Rockwells were loaded. Failing to close the door behind him, he nodded and cleared his throat. Alice waited, her lips pursed.

"I'm afraid it is about Mr. Rockwell, yes." He turned and glanced back through the open door to the darkened streets and again cleared his throat. "I, uh, you see, the chaplain was supposed to be here to help. New fella, just started. Lost, probably." He rubbed his chin still more vigorously.

Alice nodded her head, walking past Officer Dalton to close the door. Folding her hands at her waist, she waited in quiet expectation, her eyebrows slightly raised.

"Right," Dalton murmured. He twisted his hat tightly in his hands. "You see, your husband..." He broke off again and examined the ceiling for cracks in the plaster before puffing out a slow breath. "Your husband is—"

"Dead. I know." Alice nodded, staring straight into Officer Dalton's enlarged eyes.

"You do?" He leaned and glanced behind her. "Did the Chaplain already come by?"

Alice opened her mouth to speak and gave a start, covering her lips with her hand. Frank walked in through an adjoining wall to stand behind Officer Dalton. Aware of a presence behind him, Dalton turned and ventured, "Chaplain Kirkpatrick?"

Alice laughed and quickly looked down to hide her smile. The look of confusion on Dalton's face intensified, but he understood Alice's laugh well enough to know that the man standing behind him was anything but a chaplain.

Dalton faced the widow once more. "We'll, um, we'll be needing you to come and identify the body, Mrs. Rockwell." Alice glanced towards her frowning husband.

"Isn't there someone else that could do that? I'd really rather not."

Frank cleared his throat, his arms crossing in front of his chest. "I'm more than capable of identifying my own body, officer."

"Fine, fine..." Dalton began to say. The words halted in his throat. He ducked his head and raised his shoulders as if a bucket of ice water had been dumped on his neck. Shoulders still raised, he looked to Frank. "Your body?"

"My body." Frank leaned forward on his front foot and pointed at his chest. There was a certain pride in his voice for being able to talk with the authorities about his body even after death.

"This is my husband, Frank," Alice offered dryly. "He's come back."

"Oh, one of those." Dalton eyeballed Frank with cautious interest. He tentatively reached a hand out to touch the specter but Frank swiped at it as if to smack it away. Dalton jerked his hand in, the frigid chill causing a slight shiver to inch up his spine.

"The case being that you've come back..." Dalton rubbed his hands together, warming them. "Detective Clemons will come by in the morning to go over the case with you." He smiled. "It's a detective's dream to talk to the murder victim, I'll bet."

"Murder!?" Alice cried. "Who would murder Frank?"

"Yeah! Who would murder me?" repeated her husband, rubbing his chest with both hands.

"If you don't know," Dalton nodded towards them both. "I certainly can't say. I'll need to report in. And warm myself up. Who knew ghosts were so cold?" He stopped on his way out the door, sending a look of sympathy to the couple. "Sorry about your loss. Losses." He shook his head and thrust his hands deep into his pockets. "I need a drink. Good night, folks."

Alice closed the door and walked stoically to the telephone, taking up the receiver.

"Oh, Alice. Don't call Reverend Barnaby over," Frank moaned.

Alice held her finger in the rotary. "I'm not. I'm calling Sam."

"Sam? But that's a long distance call!" Frank waved his arms and circled around her, passing through counters as he did.

"You've been murdered and you're still here. I think I'll make the expense."

Frank slammed his hand onto the phone, attempting to terminate the line. It whooshed through and returned to his side. A short burst of static sounded in Alice's ear. Frank folded his arms. "Just send him a letter. Or, or a, a telegraph!"

"Don't be silly. I'm not calling him just to tell him his father's dead. I'm also going to ask him to fly up right away. His last letter said that he just can't wait to help people in the same sort of scrapes as you. This sort of a case might help his business boom. It's all about reputation, I'll bet."

"Booming business my foot. He should have gone to work for me when he got home if he wanted to make any real money." Alice continued to dial. "It's late! Don't bother him, Alice!"

"He's your son, dear. He won't be bothered. Maybe I can convince him to bring that girl he likes so much with him. His secretary." She placed her hand over the mouthpiece and kicked a heel at Frank to shush him. "Now be quiet, it's ringing."

Frank lowered his voice to a whisper. "We'll have to pay for them to fly up. Think of the expense of just one ticket, let alone two. You're a poor widow now."

Alice shook her head. Leave it to Frank to make his last ditch appeal one of finance. "That's a ridiculous statement, even for you, Frank Rockwell. He's coming, and if you don't like it, well, then you shouldn't have died."

CHAPTER TWO

Sam Rockwell unclasped the flap of a rigid amber envelope, eager to see how the photographs turned out. Pedestrians swarmed around and past him on the sidewalk outside of the L.A. Daily News. He looked back at the building and felt a pang of regret about borrowing the camera, the film, and using the developing lab.

Again.

Another favor from another war buddy. Hopefully, after this case, he'd have enough left over to at least buy the fella breakfast and a cup of coffee.

Glossy photographs reflected the intense glare of the Los Angeles sun, causing Sam to hunch over and use his broad shoulders to cast a shadow. Even when bent at the chest, Sam remained a few inches taller than the nearest bystanders. Sam was tall, but genetics provided him with such broad shoulders that no one could refer to him as lanky. He was built like a prize fighter, and boxed throughout school and during his time in the army. Had it not been for the war, his mother's fretting, and his father frowning, he might have pursued a boxing career. His trainers all raved about his instincts, and making exceptions for his older brother, Sam never lost a fair fight.

He shuffled the photos in his strong hands. Farmer's hands, his mother used to call them.

The silver and gray-scale moment-in-time showed a middle-aged woman with dark, curly hair leaning forward over a Parisian-style iron table, her blouse unbuttoned scandalously low. She was making eyes at a balding man in a loud checked jacket and white billowing pants. The man was not elderly, but clearly older than the woman, who looked to be only a few years younger than Sam's mother. The woman was clearly out of her date's league. Her husband, one Salvatore Brunetti, was nothing to look at if this was the sort of guy she was making dates with. More likely, Sam figured, the man in the photograph had stacks of lettuce and was more than willing to spend it to show Mrs. Brunetti a good time.

Getting photos of the illicit liaison was no picnic. Sam hid behind nearby palms and snapped away. It was a safe distance, but he still felt like a heel the entire time he had been there. Hopefully no one figured him for a pervert. He imagined how his father would react if he found out how he'd spent his day. Exploding like a volcano, heated lectures pouring down like lava, no doubt.

Still, work was work. For a city as large as L.A., Sam hadn't handled a Return case, ghosts, in months. The sign on his door "Specializing in Returns & The Unexplainable" felt more like a suggestion than reality.

Thumbing the top photo to the back of the pile, he examined the next; the couple was sharing a peck on the lips with flutes of champagne filling the narrow gap between their bodies. Another photo slid on top of the stack showing the bald man out of his seat and circling the table. The final picture was of him embracing the seated woman from behind, his face buried in her neck. The woman's eyes and mouth were turned up in passion. Sam felt his stomach turn.

Adultery it was, just like his client, the cuckold's sister, suspected. And all of it in broad daylight, with no regard for public decency.

Sam hated Los Angeles.

If more returning spirits didn't start showing up, he might have to rethink his business plan and move somewhere else. That is, if he could convince Amelia to come along. She was an L.A. girl, and as far as Sam was concerned, the only thing pure to be found in the city.

A bus rumbled to a stop. Sam double checked Brunetti's home address and stepped on board. He paid the fare, took a seat, and checked his watch. There'd be enough time to close the case, get paid, and walk home through Amelia's neighborhood. He walked by her brick row house as often as he could, just in case she might step out. What a coincidence.

The spine of a yellow papered novel titled, Slade Hammer and the Girl Who Screamed, creaked as Sam opened the piece of pulp fiction. Detective novel. Great research for his chosen profession. Even if the writing was only so-so.

Salvatore Brunetti and his wife lived on the third floor of a small apartment building. Sam waited for Brunetti's sister, Isabelle, on an open balcony outside a painted green door. She hired him earlier in the week. Said she'd meet him here today, ten minutes ago. He hadn't talked to her since. Sam checked his watch again.

Not wanting to miss his opportunity to still have time to "chance" upon Amelia, Sam knocked on the door. There was a shuffling from within, then a voice boomed, "I'ma coming, I'ma coming." An old-world Italian accent thick like bigoli noodles.

The door opened, pushing out the scent of garlic and olive oil. A fat, meatball of a man, stood on the threshold, staring at Sam through suspicious brown eyes. His hair was black and thinning. Sam could see sweat on his scalp and temples.

"Who are you?" Brunetti asked, adding an involuntary "ah" to the end of each word.

Sam cleared his throat to prepare his work voice. Knowing next to nothing about being a detective, he took a lesson from his father - "In business, give people the experience they expect and you'll be successful."

Frank Rockwell had meant that in the context of appearing affluent, serious, and above all else, successful in the realm of financial planning and investment. Sam believed the same would be true in the world of a private investigator and his clients. People would expect him to be like Slade Hammer, tough as nails. No nonsense. Grizzled. Drinks his milk out of a dirty glass. Sam would play the role and meet their expectations, finding a profit somewhere down the road.

"Salvatore Brunetti?" growled Sam. The fat man nodded and it occurred to Sam that his wife or sister might be inside. He didn't want to make a scene. That would delay him. "Is your wife home?"

"No. What's thees about?"

"How about your sister, Isabelle?"

Brunetti's face fell, and then darkened. "Some kinda joke?" he asked.

Sam was confused, but pressed on. He waved the envelope containing the pictures for effect. "I'm afraid your wife's been doing a little dancing on the side."

"You see my wife? Maria!"

"With my own two eyes and a camera."

"Camera!" shouted Brunetti.

"Adultery," Sam said, straight faced. A jaded gumshoe delivering the facts to a broken hearted cuckold. Fairly cut and dry work.

"Adultery!" echoed Brunetti. He was getting heated. Sam understood and looked down in spite of his act. He was sure a real sleuth would stare unflinching in the face of another's pain, like when Hammer shot the woman he loved because she worked for the Russians.

Flecks of spittle appeared on Brunetti's lips from rough, mad breaths. "My wife! You!"

It was when Brunetti bellowed "you" that Sam realized something was wrong. He looked up to see a hammy fist rocketing toward his face. The punch connected and sent a shower of damning photographs into the air, as visions of flashbulbs popped before Sam's eyes. He reeled back and tottered against the railing, getting a dizzyingly good look at three stories down. Steadying himself, he shook his head and put pressure on his eye instinctively.

"What was that for?" Sam yelled.

"You sleep-ah with my wife! I hit you again!" Brunetti moved toward Sam lethargically, the first punch seemed to have taken the pep from the fat man. A warm wind seemed to pass through Sam, and he heard excited shouting, in Italian, issuing from Isabelle, Salvatore Brunetti's sister.

Sam was grateful to see her. He didn't know what he'd have done if Brunetti would have insisted on a fight. Maybe a quick punch to the gut to sit the old man down, but Sam would have felt awful about it. Those pictures were enough of a stomach punch for any man.

Salvatore crossed himself and looked at his sister in wonder. He started to cry and reached out to embrace her. His arms passed right through. Isabelle was a Return and Sam had no idea. Some detective.

Isabelle stood still, and pantomimed a gentle stroking of what strands remained of her brother's thin hair. The big man shuddered and wept. He was awfully emotional. Everyone dies, and they move on. Sam didn't see the big deal.

Turning to Sam, Isabelle said in an accent equal to her brother's, "Thank you, Sam Rockwell. He-ah needed to know before I was gone-ah for good-ah."

"Glad to help," said Sam. "Now about my fee…"

Brother and sister looked to Sam and back to one another, shrugging their shoulders like mirror images. They began to bicker in Italian.

The street of Amelia's row house was haunted by a lovesick ghost named Sam Rockwell, nursing a shiner and eating his payment, a thick loaf of garlic bread.

Amelia lived by herself on money willed to her by her parents. They died in an automobile accident while Amelia was attending Mills College. Though she would trade it all just for them to come back a few days as Returns, Amelia had more than enough money to provide her a comfortable life through old age. Like Sam, she hadn't settled down like the rest of the post-war men and women.

Sam reveled in the overpowering feeling that at any second, Amelia may suddenly appear. But she didn't.

Must not be home, he decided.

He thought about buzzing her doorbell, but worried that he'd come across too desperate. He'd asked her to work for him when she showed interest in helping Returns, though paying her for her one day a week in his office ate up most all of his extra money. Still, enough remained for the occasional date which, for now, had to be good enough.

"Marriage," his father would say, "is for men who can provide a home and good life to their spouse. Remember that, Samuel."

Yes, sir.

Disappointed and tired, Sam decided to walk the several blocks to his office at the Baker Building. He passed a group of boys playing baseball in the street.

CRACK! The smack of ash crushing horsehide reverberated among the cars and town homes.

One of those kids might have a future in the big leagues. Sam followed the arc of a well hit ball as it clattered against the metal rails of a nearby fire escape. The pack of boys ran ahead and vainly tried jumping up to grasp the bottom rung of a rusting ladder leading down from the escape, but it was too high.

"Hey, Mister!" a boy shouted at Sam. "You're tall, lift me up to fetch our ball."

"Please," said Sam, stuffing the last piece of bread in his mouth and hoisting the boy up by his armpits. The child ignored the invitation to use his manners, using instead Sam's swollen eye as a final step as he grabbed hold of the ladder. Sam gave a muffled "Ow!" from behind the lump of bread. The rest of the pack cheered in triumph and Sam strolled onward.

"Hey, Mister! I don't wanna jump down that far. Please."

"Glad to help," Sam said, scratching his head and turning back toward the fire escape.

Sam's seasoned leather shoes brushed the top of each stair, sounding like a broom sweeping away sand as he marched up the Baker Building steps to his office. Nearly halfway up his final flight, his foot caught on a riser. He reacted quickly, regaining his balance by grabbing the handrail with one hand and baluster with the other.

The sudden movement left his face pounding. Brunetti's punch was beginning to catch up with him.

After scolding the unusually high step, he began to deliberately raise each foot an exaggerated extra six inches before placing it back onto solid tread with a slap. He might look like Harpo Marx, but his head didn't need the further jarring a fall would cause.

Down the end of the hall, Sam saw through the frosted glass of his office that the lights were on. It was nearly eight.

Sam's heart skipped a beat.

Maybe Amelia was still working, waiting to see how the Brunetti investigation turned out. Maybe she just wanted to see him. He was certainly eager to see her.

A wide grin crossed Sam's face. He immediately repented of the expression, his hand shooting up to his swollen right cheek. Sam let loose a hushed and mottled stream of profanity, scrubbed clean of anything truly objectionable by the religious upbringing his mother provided.

Reaching the door, his thoughts were clouded with the storm that was Salvatore Brunetti. For a man his size, he had no business owning a left hook anywhere near as quick as what landed on his face. Sam examined the gold and black lettering, his high school colors, painted on the door. They were courtesy of one of the few cases that blessed him with anything left over.

S. ROCKWELL, PRIVATE INVESTIGATOR
Returns & the Unexplainable Welcomed

'Returns' was the accepted term used for dead folks who came back, usually due to sufficiently important unfinished business. Who made the determination on who Returned or not was still a hot topic among theologians. Sam was fine with leaving it to them.

Angels or apostles, whoever called the shots upstairs didn't seem to have any rhyme or reason Sam could make out. Not that he dealt with a large sample size. Still, the few times a Return actually made his way into the office, they weren't exactly asking him to save the world. Often cases were as simple and jejune as an executive returning to share the code for his wall safe with his business partner. There was the time a fellow returned to get Sam to tell a jury that his death was a suicide, and not poisoning from his wife. That one felt important. Sam didn't have the heart to ask the widow for payment.

Returns were common enough, but Return cases were a different story. He may as well have specialized in time travel or space exploration for all the business he'd gotten. When a Return did show up to hire him, it was usually like the Isabelle Brunetti job—something he just stumbled into.

Bills kept coming, and he needed to try his hand at real detective work until more Returns walked through his door. Technically, Sam had no formal training in any sort of police work. He had read a lot of books on the subject, however.

Grabbing the door knob, Sam turned and found it locked. There was a faint stirring from inside. His heart soared, happy that Amelia was still in the office. He rapped the glass with his knuckle and called out with a voice far cheerier than his bruised face would suggest. "Open up Amelia, it's me."

"You have a key."

"Maybe I should've said it's Cary Grant," Sam muttered to himself.

Fumbling in his pocket, he found the keys and set them in the lock. Sam flung the door open as if he were casting his jacket onto the bed. Swinging nearly half way into the room, the door then hit Amelia's desk, causing it to reverberate back into Sam's expecting hand.

Space was tight, but rent was also high. You learned to make do.

Holding the door against the desk, Sam turned his body sideways and squeezed into his office. He lost more than a couple of flesh and blood clients over the tight fix. Sam figured any Returns would just walk through the door. It was a great plan, if he could find any Returns to hire him.

A larger place to do business was on the list of things Sam wanted, when he had the money. The current space was clearly once a store room or supply closet. There was room for Sam's desk, a pair of spartan swivel chairs, a water cooler, and a brass coat rack. There was no room for the filing cabinets, potted plants, or Amelia's desk. They were squeezed in all the same.

Amelia Martin sat behind Sam's desk, reading a late edition of the L.A. Daily News. She liked to sit in Sam's place whenever he was away, avoiding the guaranteed fright that accompanied the door slamming into her desk. Her green eyes stayed on the newsprint as Sam sauntered the short way from door to desk.

Hanging his jacket and hat on the coat rack, he hardened his voice, attempting to make it sound less like Bob Hope and more like Humphrey Bogart. "Hop outta my seat, 'melia."

"Cut the act," Amelia said, playfully swatting Sam with her

newspaper. She noticed the yellowish bruise smeared across his face. A frown bent her pert red lips. Moving with a grace Sam found irresistible, she bit her lower lip and seated herself on the opposite side of the desk, waiting for an explanation.

Sam collapsed into his newly opened chair, then stood again and absentmindedly pulled a dog eared pulp paperback from his pocket. He tossed the book on the table. "If we're going to make it in this business, I have to be sure to sound the part. Hard boiled and all." He knocked on his head.

"Things got a little rough tonight," noted Amelia with a slight hesitation in her voice. She eyed Sam's swelling face. "You poor thing, let me get you something to drink." She glided behind the desk and pulled a nearly empty whiskey bottle from a drawer.

"Just water is fine, Amelia. Bottle's nearly empty and I don't have any more apple juice to fill it again." Sam didn't enjoy the taste of alcohol. Never had. But, he figured that people expected gritty detectives to drink. Profusely. All a part of the act.

Amelia fetched the water and leaned backwards against the desk, standing next to Sam's chair and looking down at him.

"Thanks" Sam said, taking a swallow. "If anyone comes in, we'll say it's vodka."

"So what happened?" Amelia asked. "I thought this was supposed to be easy money."

"Salvatore Brunetti happened." Sam waved his palm over his swollen cheek. "In a true Italian fit of rage."

"So his wife was an adulterer. How sad. But why did he take it out on you?"

"The fat slug thought I was confessing to being his wife's lover. His English comprehension could stand some improvement. I expected blubbering tears. The punch caught me off guard is all."

Amelia tapped her shoes. "Didn't his sister tell him you were coming with the news?"

"No. She didn't tell him anything. Get this," Sam said, leaning in toward Amelia and taking in the floral scent of her perfume. "Remember how I said she didn't want to hurt the sensitive soul's feelings or cause a rift in case the wife was innocent?"

"She hired us based on her suspicions," Amelia said, nodding.

"Right. Only she didn't say a word about it to Tubby Marciano because she was a Return." Sam watched as Amelia's eyes lit up. "She showed up after the punch landed and started hollering in Italian. Probably telling him to stop and giving him the story."

Working with Returns is what drew Amelia to Sam in the first place. She was eager to help those whose life had ended somehow just short. Animated, she asked, "Did he seem glad to see her?"

"Very. Couldn't stop crying. I didn't get it."

Amelia frowned. "You should. I certainly do." She examined her fingernails and worked at her lip in silence. Taking a deep breath, she watched Sam closely. "I wish you could find more Return cases."

"There just aren't enough people dying in our city," Sam said absently, his hand gingerly patting his puffing eye.

"What a terrible thing to say!" Amelia and Sam both said at the same time, Amelia at Sam and Sam at himself. Sam gave a half smile and locked eyes with Amelia.

A long whistle blew from Amelia's lips as she examined Brunetti's handy-work. "He sure did a number on you. I thought you said you knew how to fight. You can make a lot more money as a boxer than a punching bag detective."

Sam downed another gulp of water, trying hard not to return her smile. "Oh, don't sound too impressed. I can hold my own when I need to. I was a top notch boxer." He raised his fists, as if proving the point. "High School, College, the Army. Sure, I know how to knock someone's block off. Not to mention the tricks you learn from having an older brother."

"I certainly hope so." Amelia skipped to retrieve her purse, ready to call it an evening. "The fighting is the one thing from those novels that you can't fake. That, and how to investigate a crime scene."

The door banged abruptly against Amelia's desk, slamming itself closed again. The sole advantage of the stunted and obstructed entrance was the time it gave Sam to make an all-important first impression. Knowing the drill, Amelia rushed to look busy at a file cabinet while Sam swiftly hid the detective novel in a desk drawer. He stood up, in character, to greet whatever customer stood confusedly outside. The hour was late and this was obviously not a return case or they'd have just walked through solid wood, but money is money.

A young woman, vivacious with a red silk dress and black fur, re-opened the door at a slower pace, pushing it until it gently tapped against Amelia's desk. A cascading sheen of blond hair shone behind her as she stepped inside.

Alison Bouvier. Sam's heart quickened at the sight of her. If he played this right, Bouvier might provide a decent paying job. He crossed his arms and leaned against his desk, inviting the rich young socialite to come in.

"Sorry about the noise, doll," said Sam in full noire style. "Necessary precaution. In my line of work it's best not to let anyone sneak up on you."

Nodding for her to come over, he poured the last contents of his whiskey bottle into a heavy glass tumbler, baring his teeth as he emptied the glass. He wanted it gone before she could smell that it was apple juice.

Sam kept acquaintance with a man who worked at the Hillside Hotel, where Bouvier was staying. He would get a telephone call whenever a problem popped up that his services might aid. In exchange for a percentage, of course. Miss Bouvier had lost a family necklace, worth no small amount. Sam had hurried to find her in the hotel bar when his contact called him with the tip. The initial meeting went well. Bouvier seemed thrilled to speak with a real-life private investigator, "just like in the movies." Sam didn't feel the interview was his best performance, but here the lady was, no doubt ready to hire.

"Oh, I understand," said Bouvier, standing just inside the office. "Your job must be very dangerous. You're very brave." She blushed, her eyes lingering for a moment on his bruise. "I wanted to come by and talk to you further about that missing necklace."

"Sure," said Sam, adding a bit of extra gravel to his voice. "Fifty bucks up front plus expenses. Any leads you can tell me about?"

Bouvier stood in front of Sam, almost too close for polite company. She reddened further, turning her head down to the side.

"Oh," she said softly, "You see, I found it. The necklace, I mean. It was wrapped in some clothing I'd already packed. I guess I missed it."

Sam's heart fell but he didn't crack. No necklace job, but

maybe she had something else for him.

"I'm sorry to hear that, doll," Sam said. He stared into her large blue eyes and added, "I was looking forward to working with you."

The girl let out a warm breath and said, "I'd be happy to pay you for the time you've already spent with me."

Sam channeled a pulp detective. "I wasn't looking forward to the money. I was looking forward to working with you."

"Oh," Bouvier said, somewhat breathlessly it seemed to Sam. A rush of blood painted her cheeks carnation pink. She stepped closer, erasing the final remaining amount of personal space. Pressing her body against Sam's, eyes looking up expectantly. "Well, I did mean to come and... thank you, after all."

Sam's eyes flashed, panicked by Miss Bouvier's dusky blue bedroom eyes whispering promises of sin. This was precisely the place his childhood Sunday School Proverbs warned him of. He glanced at Amelia and gulped at the apocalyptic glare leveled against him.

I was looking forward to working with you.

Sam mentally kicked himself. The line was exactly what any fictional detective would have said. And he knew what any granite-faced detective worth his revolver would do with Miss Bouvier next. But Sam Rockwell, Returns and the Unexplainable detective, in love with his secretary?

Not so much.

He was cornered and needed to find a way out without breaking his act. Word would get around and he would never get another case. A line from the novel in his desk sprang into his mind like a kid on a pogo stick. "You don't want to get mixed up with a guy like me, baby."

Miss Bouvier took a step backward, clearly confused by the contradiction. "But you just said-"

Sam laughed nervously, his voice back to its natural, Bob Hope-like tone. "Sorry, find yourself a man who can take care of you the way you deserve. It's too dangerous being around me. I work alone." He shot the words out like a terrified machine gun.

Hurriedly, he pushed against Bouvier's back, squeezing her through the door. She spun around one last time in the hallway and stared at Sam. Bewilderment bordering on incredulity.

"Goodbye, Ms. Bouvier. I'm glad you found your necklace!" shouted Sam, closing the door on her. He leaned against it, assuring no re-entry until the awkward clicking of Miss Bouvier's heels could no longer be heard.

Amelia was once again seated at Sam's desk, her arms across her chest and one eyebrow raised as she swiveled slightly back and forth.

Sam guffawed. "I guess I don't know my own charm. My mother always said I looked like Gregory Peck. Who knew I was so irresistible?" Suddenly somber, he added, "Sorry, Amelia."

With an air of mocking indifference, Amelia shrugged. "You don't owe me an apology, Mr. Rockwell. I'm only your secretary after all." She tilted her head and smiled, making sure that every one of her white teeth was on display.

"Oh, come on, Amelia. You know I only hired you so I could be near you without having to spring for dinner."

A smile spread across her lips in spite of her tense posture.

"We've got a big future together," Sam said, "I hope."

"You hope?" said Amelia, reaching for her coat, ready to call it an evening. "I think a man should have the courage to ask if there's a big future ahead."

"Oh, I'm very cowardly." He looked down at his shoes with a look of helpless devastation.

Amelia laughed and shook her head.

Sam's smile returned to the room and danced across his face. He didn't notice the pain from Brunetti's punch. His eyes twinkled. "But suppose I did ask you about a big future, how would you answer?"

"Only one way to find out, Sam Rockwell."

A fleet of butterflies soared over Sam's stomach like B-17 bombers, dropping payloads of adrenaline. He wanted to find out, wanted the answer to be yes. He opened his mouth to reply when the shrill ring of the telephone sounded from Amelia's desk. She gave Sam a quizzical look and picked up the receiver.

"Oh, hello Mrs. Rockwell." Concern knit worries onto her brow.

CHAPTER THREE

On the first night of his death, Frank Rockwell went to bed irritated. His life, which he now viewed in the past tense, had been one of firm control. He prided himself on never deviating from his routine, his disciplines.

But the night of his murder saw a change to all that. He couldn't pour himself a nightcap or light a cigar. It was a bitter reality that those two worldly reliefs would be of no use to a ghost. Frank was unable to recall a time he would have welcomed them more.

What luck.

Cigars and drinks he could move past. What really steamed him were the sharp little reminders that he wasn't a man for this world any longer. He tried to slip into his pajamas and found that only his spectral jacket and hat were removable.

That was odd. To make matters worse, his hat—a favorite, was gone. It disappeared through the floor when he threw it earlier. Perhaps he acted a bit rashly and let his anger get the best of him, but Alice wasn't exactly making him feel like a cherished husband. The hat might well be somewhere in Australia for all he knew.

Frustrations mounted.

Water couldn't be run. Light switches were un-switchable. His covers were impervious to being turned down. Each new failure stung Frank like a paper cut, never expected and bleeding more than it seemed it should. By bedtime, Frank was profusely irked as he lingered in his bathroom, swiping impotently at his toothbrush.

Finally, he surrendered to his new reality and lay down on top of Alice's favorite quilt, waiting for his wife to finish her shower and join him in bed. She came into the room and smiled at him through a yawn. Frank got up from the bed and walked toward her as she sat and combed her hair in front of her dresser mirror. He leaned down for a kiss and she inclined her cheek to receive it, the same as every night. Frank's phantom lips brought ice to Alice's warm skin and she gave out a shout and shrank back with a jolt.

"No more of that, Frank. It's like having a cube of ice pressed against me."

Frank tossed his hands up. "You say it like I chose to become a ghost and miss my pot roast!" He crossed his arms and pouted.

"I'm sorry, dear." Alice slipped into bed by the soft glow of her nightstand lamp but sat up quickly. "Are you tired, Frank? I mean, can you feel tired?"

Frank seemed to float back on top of the bed, careful not to touch her. "Not particularly," he answered. "I don't know if I can sleep or not."

Alice clicked the lamp off. "I suppose you'll find out tonight, darling. I can say with certainty that I need to go to sleep. I can hardly keep my eyes open."

In the darkened silence, Frank shifted onto his side, propping an elbow up to rest his head. "You don't feel like talking, Alice? I was murdered after all."

"I'm sorry you were murdered, dear," Alice mumbled, her voice trailing as slumber approached. The couple rolled onto their sides, facing one another. They moved in for a perfunctory good night kiss. Alice's eyelids fluttered open to see Frank's face, eyes still closed and lips puckered, inches away. She pulled back to avoid the chill. Frank caught on, and the two issued a twin pair of awkward and apologetic laughs.

"Alice, I wanted to talk with you about the reason I Returned. My part in the affair, as it was. It's a story that begins long ago. You see—"

"I'm sorry," Alice interrupted. "I'm too tired for a long talk. Can you make it quick or can it wait until morning?"

Frank soured. "Good night, dear." He scooched himself to the edge of the bed and rose his voice purposefully loud. "I'll stay here on the edge for a while so you don't get woken up by an ice bath."

Alice jumped at the volume of Frank's voice and resettled. "We'll have plenty of time to talk about all of that tomorrow when Sam gets home," she offered through a yawn. "He's flying in first thing with Amelia."

Frank wore the exaggerated look of his deepest grievance. It was a look Alice was familiar with, but Frank realized that in the darkness it would offer her no clues. He held his tongue, but only for so long. Soon a series of deep breaths and pitiful sighs sounded from his side of the bed. He wanted Alice to ask him what was wrong, so he'd have an opportunity to tell her why he Returned. The cadence of her breathing made it clear that such questions wouldn't come until morning. Frank let out one last annoyed sigh, folded his arms, and stared at the walls and ceiling. Alice slept on.

Blue moonlight entered through the bedroom window, casting a sprawling cross on the far wall. Frank had seen the effect of the light on the window panes before. Tonight, the shadow was symbolic. He saw it as an 'X'. He'd been rubbed off. The mark of change.

Life as Frank knew it had come to an end. Alice was gone from him, or soon would be. Sam was coming, happily. Frank disliked the fact that his son was only coming to take a job where success meant seeing him departed permanently. With Sam now a delusional private investigator, the family business would be sold. Alice was no investment adviser and Sam resisted every attempt to work for his father, the influence of Sam's older brother Elijah.

Frank chuckled at the idea of seeing Elijah again. It was a nice thought. He made a note to remind Alice of the fact. She would be happy to hear it, and maybe he could arrange for Elijah to Return again to talk Sam into taking over the business. But Sam was probably right about Elijah having moved on for good.

Everything Frank knew had changed or was changing. With

the exception of standing, sitting, or lying down, basic physical contact was now beyond his ability. Others said they felt coldness when they came into contact with him. At least they felt something. Frank could only feel himself. He knew he was lying on his back by perspective, but he could not sense the materiality of the quilt or mattress beneath him. He felt no hunger, though a desire to eat came to him when he saw dinner on the table. That was torturous. He dreaded the coming of his accustomed late night snack. Could he sleep? Did he even need to any longer? He determined to close his eyes and make an attempt, if only to pass the time until tomorrow.

Whether he slept or not, Frank didn't know. Moments after he closed his eyes, he reopened them and found he was no longer with Alice or in their bed.

Angels and the dead weaved in and out of the teeming Pearly Gates Administration Building. Voices and footfalls echoed off the polished white marble floors, carrying upward to a gilded vaulted ceiling, shining brightly from what seemed a mile overhead.

Frank stood in the middle of a great main hall, gleaming with deep dark grains of mahogany and milky white marble. He was back again.

Had the murderer been caught? And before he was able to see Sam? There were things he needed to tell Alice one last time before he could go back. He should have just told her straight away instead of dancing around the subject and needling her to treat him more somberly. Maybe his killer was already caught, and his time was up. He needed to find out.

He joined a queue of the departed as they waited within red velvet ropes. Their style of dress indicated that some of the dead had been in the Administration Building for decades or more. Fitting. The building felt to Frank one part museum and one part post office. There was nothing as slow, costly, and inefficient as a bureaucracy.

It was clear to Frank that he wasn't in heaven yet. It was too far from perfect. Someone needed to whip this place into shape. He looked eagerly for the spectral body of Calvin Coolidge. Silent Cal could have the place fixed up in no time. Frank gave a half-frown, half-scowl when the former President was nowhere to be seen.

The click-clump of heavy boots sounded. Frank turned to see a man wearing the double breasted gray and yellow fringed coat of a Confederate States officer take a place in line behind him.

"Good day to you, sir," The soldier said with a Dixie voice from behind a magnificently bushy mustache.

Frank gave a disdainful sideways glance and folded his arms in dismissal. Where was General Sherman when you needed him?

The two men stood in silence for some time. The Confederate pulled tightly on a white cavalry glove. "I observe from your finery, sir, that you are of the more recently deceased."

Pretending not to hear, Frank stared directly ahead. But his curiosity soon overtook him and he turned to face the rebel. "How did you die? The front of your uniform looks spotless, so I assume you were shot in the back while running from Old Glory."

The Confederate chuckled softly. "A cannonball took me clean off my horse and straight here."

"I would've thought cannonballs left larger holes."

"I assure you they do. However everyone gets cleaned up upon entering these halls. No grievous wounds to be seen, your clothing somehow laundered and smelling of lavender. It's not heaven, or even Georgia, but I was glad for it after that war."

"I'm glad your little costume is all nice and shiny. I noticed the smell the first time I was here. I'm not an idiot." He turned to face forward again, but soon looked back at the Confederate, eying him up and down. "Your side lost, by the way." Frank was delighted by this final jab. Served the turncoat right.

The soldier's gloved hand grabbed Frank's shoulder, not challengingly but gently, seeking Frank's attention. Frank spun to face the man, ready to give the rebel a yell of his own.

"Where do you get off?" Frank scolded.

Heads turned at the outburst. Two angels in dark blue uniforms began to move from their post near elevator doors but stopped when the Confederate waved them off.

"I'm afraid I don't comprehend your meaning," the officer drawled while stroking his mustache. He gave a dismissing smile, diffusing the crowd's attention. Lowering his voice, he continued, "but if you've been here once before, it is to your advantage to hear me speak on the matter."

"I don't make a habit of listening to communists, or rebels, or anyone else living or dead who made himself an enemy of the United States!"

"He that harkeneth unto counsel is wise," the Confederate answered softly, extending his hand to Frank. "I'm Captain Jeremiah Buford."

Frank stared blankly at the proffered hand and shook it, more from protocol than pleasure.

"Am I to understand," said Buford, "that you were once already sent back to Earth following your demise?"

"And what's that to you?" demanded Frank.

"I once was as well. Did they tell you why you were to be sent back?"

"No." Frank frowned. The rebel had his interest.

"We are the same then—" began the gray shade.

"Now hold your cotton picking horses," Frank protested, his finger wagging at Buford. "I love my country! I'm a decent American. I'm no pinko traitor rebel!"

"We are the same," Buford growled through clenched teeth, "in the similitude of circumstance following our deaths. When you returned to this grand hall and not on an elevator up, I say with surety that the decision to send you back has been reconsidered."

"You mean I won't see Alice again?" Frank's face was pale.

"Your sweetheart, I take you to mean? No, not until it's her turn to pass through. I assume you'll both take the elevator up."

His first visit had come and gone in moments. Frank found a place in a line marked Returns and was sent back almost immediately by the harried clerk. Had his Return been an error, then? Frank clasped the Confederate's arm, and with an imploring whisper asked, "What should I do?"

The old soldier leaned in close. "They are very trusting up here, by nature, you understand? A man can use that to his advantage, or he can get swept away with feelings of pious duty and be stuck waiting for whatever reason I'm still in this forsaken lobby. I know now what I'd do with the opportunity you now have. Convince them that sending you back was not in error. Make them to understand that your return is of the utmost importance."

"Well, it is!" Frank insisted.

"I am glad to know it. No clerical work is entirely free of errors, even here," said Buford. He offered Frank his hand again. "I wish you all the best of luck, sir."

Frank took the hand and shook it vigorously. He had taken for granted that he could actually feel things at the administration building, the sensation was so natural. He now reveled in the handshake and his realization of this regained sensation.

"Next!" yelled a voice ahead. Frank realized that meant him. The line ended at a long counter with small windows, like a bank. He walked to the waiting clerk.

"I'm Frank Rockwell."

"Are you Frank Rockwell?" asked the clerk.

"Yes. I just said so."

"I have a message for Frank Rockwell."

"Well, let me have it!"

The clerk searched through a stack of carbon paper. Frank turned sideways and leaned his elbow against the counter. He watched as the Confederate approached the window next to him.

"Any news of what is to become of Jeremiah Buford?" asked the officer.

"Sorry, Captain," the clerk replied. "Nothing yet. The boys are still searching for an opportunity for you. You'll get to move on before Judgment day. Probably."

Buford sighed and nodded at the clerk, and then to Frank, who returned the gesture just as his own clerk rattled a sheet of yellow paper with both hands.

"Here it is," the clerk triumphed. "It says you're to report to Validations and Departures. Thirty six doors down. A courier will show you."

Frank gasped as a short man with a red jacket and matching trousers popped into being next to him.

"This way, sir!" the courier said, saluting with white gloves.

Following the red jacketed fellow to a frosted glass door, Frank entered at the short courier's beckoning. He was gone before Frank could fully close the door. The room had several sofas and a reception desk. A woman in a white dress sat behind a typewriter while another clerk, harried and rocking back and forth slightly, sat with head in hands on one of the waiting room couches.

"You're the fellow who I saw yesterday, aren't you?" Frank asked the man.

"I am," said the clerk, looking up through a pair of bifocals. "I made the right decision sending you back, didn't I Mr. Rockwell? When I checked you in?"

"Don't be silly," Frank said, inwardly wincing at the barb the moment he gave it. Perhaps it would be better to ingratiate this man to sooner get back to Alice.

"Oh good, good. My supervisor will send you on and let me off with a warning if it's the case."

So it was the supervisor who held the keys. Frank no longer felt bad about being curt with the clerk. Whoever this middle manager was, Frank would work him into letting him back home. Barely a minute went by before the secretary announced that he and the clerk were ready to be seen.

Frank led the way.

"I'm a man of business," Frank said to the clerk trailing behind him. "Let me handle this."

The clerk nodded a relieved assent and the two entered the office, taking chairs before a great desk. A nameplate reading Philip Eamon faced the visitors. Mr. Eamon himself sat with his back turned to his visitors, reading through a folder intently. His black suit blended precisely with the black leather chair.

Eamon turned his chair suddenly, taking no notice of Frank or the clerk. Instead, he stared at the papers on his desk. He seemed eminently distracted by his work.

Frank knew the trick and stared back with a stone face, inviting the man to test him. Eamon lifted his head from the paperwork and looked up evenly at the two men. His eyes dazzled a moment, as if he were truly unaware they had arrived. Frank rolled his eyes and grunted dismissively.

"Mr. Rockwell," Eamon said, pushing a stack of papers to the side of the desk. He spoke with a dapper English accent. "This hat belongs to you, I believe?"

Frank glanced at his hat and then locked eyes with the man in front of him. Reaching across the desk, he took the hat without thanks. Eamon nodded and then frowned at the clerk, still shaking in his seat.

"So, you're British," said Frank, rolling his eyes. "That's wonderful. I'm here for business and you're ready to offer me a pot of tea, I suppose."

Eamon sat stiffly in his chair, eyes wide. He drummed his fingers on the desk. "A spot of tea wasn't on the docket, Mr. Rockwell. There's no time for it. And, I'm not British as you suppose. I was stationed in England as a guardian angel for three centuries. I picked up their way of speaking. That's hardly the sort of thing to get upset about."

"Well?" Frank folded his arms and furrowed his brow. Eamon, taken aback by Frank's curt impatience, cleared his throat.

"The fellow here," Eamon nodded toward the clerk, "has exhibited an unfortunate track record of working too quickly. It's understandable. We're positively overwhelmed. But, this makes him prone to error."

The clerk reburied his head into his hands.

"I have reason to believe," Eamon said, "that your Return was just such an error." He flicked at a piece of loose paper on his desk. Frank sensed that Eamon was looking to wrap things up quickly and return to his business. Perhaps the key would be to hold things up.

"I thought Heaven didn't make mistakes."

"HE doesn't make mistakes." Eamon's eyes shot upwards. "But those of us working in his employ sometimes do." He looked at the clerk. "Some of us more than others, sad to say."

A pitiful groan, as if he had swallowed a pint of tobacco juice, erupted from the clerk. Frank shot a contemptuous look at the noise, holding his glare until he was sure Eamon saw it.

"In life I was never a man to allow repeated failures in business. I wish you all the best in your corrective measures." Frank began to lift himself from his seat, the interview over.

"Just a few more moments." Eamon watched Frank slowly sit back down and gave a forced, fractional smile. "I'd like to be finished as well, but not yet. You told our clerk here that your return was... important?" His voice rose as he finished the sentence.

"Of course my return was important!" snapped Frank.

Eamon recoiled slightly. "Did you tell him why it was important?"

Frank scraped his cuticles against his silk suit jacket, examining them with the disinterest of a Senator speaking to someone else's voter. "I assumed he knew."

"He took your word on the matter and sent you back," informed Eamon, "without filing any of the necessary forms."

The clerk lifted his head and pleaded, "We were so backed up and he seemed very sure of things—"

"Are you questioning my story?" Frank cut him off.

"Oh no, sir!" exclaimed the clerk.

Letting out a sigh, Eamon rose from his seat and paced behind his desk, his hands clasped behind his back. "Procedures are procedures, and must be followed. I'm sure a man such as you understands?"

"I'll fill out your forms." Frank reached for a fountain pen on the desk. "How soon will I be sent back?"

Eamon stopped pacing and stole a glance at a row of clocks on his back wall. "I'm afraid I have to establish just what was so important that you should Return?"

Frank nodded with a grave countenance. His chance to see Alice again was now. He licked his lips furtively and levered himself out of his chair. "Preventing World War Three."

The clerk and Mr. Eamon looked to Frank in hushed wonder.

"I suppose we'd better get you back quickly, then," Eamon said.

The interview was over.

CHAPTER FOUR

The cab driver was thin as a finish nail and seemed always on the verge of falling out of his seat. All of the man's strength and focus was bent on preventing his steel beast from hurling him from the saddle. Soaring down residential streets, the vehicle nearly went airborne when white-walled tires met a maple root pushing through the pavement.

"This would do for a getaway," Sam said to Amelia, "but I didn't need to get to my parent's house this fast."

Amelia was pale. One hand pressed firmly against the car ceiling while her other hand crumpled the shoulder of Sam's suit like discarded wrapping paper. The ride was frightening, but Sam thrilled at Amelia's touch, never so happy to be fearful.

The driver was silent. He asked his patrons their destination in a backwoods drawl at the airport and then clammed up once his battle with the cab started. Sam counted seven occasions when he would have grabbed the wheel from its trembling master if he sat close enough.

"We're almost there," Sam said to Amelia, his voice vibrating slightly. "Maybe his wife is in labor and we're the last customers until he gets to the hospital."

Amelia nodded, the worry betraying her smile. Sam's long legs protested against the backseat confinement that followed their morning flight. He rubbed his knees, then his face. The swelling was down. Just a deep purple knot on his cheekbone remained. "I'll be annoyed if we sat through this drive just to die as soon as we get in my old neighborhood."

A group of barefoot boys clad in bathing suits scattered at the taxi's blitzkrieg. Amelia gasped as the boys ran pell-mell from the middle of the road. Spinning around, Sam watched as the boys threw their soggy towels after the cab in protest. The rawboned wheel-man seemed oblivious.

Sam met Amelia's disbelieving eyes. "Must have thought they were Returns."

"That's not funny," Amelia said.

Leaning toward the driver, Sam couldn't keep the grin from his face. He tapped the man on the shoulder. "Been a cabby long? I hear the trick is letting your passengers live long enough to pay you."

Sam hoped the quip would at the very least get the driver to slow down and converse. Instead, he replied with a jittery nod. The car accelerated abruptly, sending Sam back into his seat. He gripped Amelia's shoulder. "I don't think the fella's mule back home went quite this fast."

Stretching forward, Sam again patted the driver's wispy shoulder. He pointed out a shabby house, once tan but now only dirty. "That's the place," he said, nearly tumbling into the front seat as the car jerked to a skidding halt. The cabby's lead foot showed equal favor to both the gas and brake pedals.

Pulling Amelia out of the backseat, Sam rushed through the process of retrieving luggage from the trunk. He handed the waif of a driver his payment. "Nice day to walk home from work, don't you think?"

Watching the cab drive off until he was sure any pedestrians on the block were safe, Sam turned his attention to Amelia. She stared at the tan house, tilting her head to match the angle it leaned. Sam took the suitcase from her hand. "Let's go meet my mother and ghostly Father, shall we?"

Amelia started for the house before Sam caught her attention with the clearing of his throat. "The house is a few blocks down yet. I felt like we beat some pretty tall odds just making it this far. Didn't want to press our luck any further."

The pair walked side by side. Amelia folded her hands and admired the trees and flower gardens. Sam held a suitcase in each hand and another under each arm. It was only a few blocks, but he was already second guessing his decision to walk. The suitcases seemed to be filling with rocks at every step.

"The farthest north I'd been before landing at SeaTac was Sacramento," Amelia said, glancing at Sam's arms as they strained to keep the load together. "Let me take one of those."

"I've got it," grunted Sam. He turned his body away from

Amelia's outstretched hand.

Amelia twitched her lips. "It's very sweet of you to bring me on the case."

"I had enough for a round-fare trip and figured I could just as easily buy two one-way tickets."

"Your mother paid for the tickets."

"She paid for them, but I bought 'em. I made sure they were one-way only. I hope you like it here." Sam stopped to put down the suitcases, adjusting his grip.

Amelia paused with him. "Are you sure I can't—"

"No, I've got it."

"So we're stuck in Tacoma?"

Sam smiled. "I booked a return trip for you on Sunday. Should be long enough to see some sites, go to the funeral. Hopefully this will all go smooth and I'll be right on your heels."

"Why did you bring me along, Sam?" Amelia asked, stopping beneath the shade of maple leaves. Sam put down his burdens, happy for the break but tentative about the coming conversation.

"You're my secretary. I might need you for the case."

"Ha. Ha. Tell me the truth."

"I thought maybe," Sam put his hands on his hips and let out a breath. "Maybe you should meet my father before he's gone for good. And because it's pretty here. I wanted you to see that too." Sam pointed to the snow covered peaks of Mount Rainier. The white blazed brilliantly in the summer sun.

"Just look at Mt. Rainier," Amelia said. "It is pretty here. Beautiful."

"We all just call it 'the mountain.' Once you've seen it," he paused to pick up the luggage, "there's no sense in calling it anything else. What other mountain could it be?"

Amelia snatched a suitcase away from Sam and walked ahead before he could protest. She called over her shoulder, "Did you have one of those dreams again after the Brunetti Return touched you?"

"Yeah." Sam jogged to catch up to Amelia and reached for her suitcase. She quickly pulled away from his outstretched fingers.

"Fall in, soldier," ordered Amelia.

Sam laughed and joined Amelia stride for stride, giving up on retrieving her luggage. He didn't feel nearly as chivalrous as when they first started walking, but the relief he felt in his arms was welcome.

"Tell me about the dream."

"The Brunetti brother and sister were kids playing in Italy, and she asked me to help him when his viper of a wife showed up. Pretty much like how it played out in real life."

"Did it end the same?"

Sam pointed to a white house on the next block. "Almost there. Yeah, the same old messenger showed up and asked me to sign some papers. Then I woke up."

Amelia wiped her brow. "I wonder what would happen if you ever signed?"

"Beats me. He'd probably tell me it was needed in triplicate and I'd wake up before the last one. It's probably nothing but my imagination from all those novels I read."

"I think there's something more to it. It happens every time you touch a Return."

"Maybe," Sam shrugged. "We've arrived."

The couple stepped onto a meticulously kept lawn, vibrant

green in defiance of the summer sun. A black Cadillac gleamed in front of the carriage house. Sam and his older brother Elijah used the building for a criminal den in neighborhood games of cops and robbers. They weren't allowed to touch the car.

Amelia patted a great oak tree rooted along a garden footpath and looked up at the white Queen Anne home towering above her. "This is more what I had in mind. With what you'd told me about your parents, I was surprised when we stopped in front of that old tan shack."

Sam led Amelia to the front door. "My Father's done pretty well for himself."

"I'll say."

The door opened and for the second day in a row, Sam found his reflexes not up to the speed of his rival. His mother pulled him into her embrace. Alice Rockwell clung to her son tightly, pinching Sam's shirt collar into his neck and laughing from a deep spring of joy.

Breathing in her familiar scented jasmine and almond perfume, Sam gently pushed Alice away. She was as beautiful as the bright woman he remembered from his youth. Age gave her a certain nobility but not at the expense of liveliness.

Amelia smiled quietly and waited for an introduction

"Hello, mother," Sam said. "It's great to see you. This is Amelia."

"Oh, yes, your secretary." She gave a wink devoid of all subtlety and took Amelia by both hands. "It's so nice to meet you. We—I have a room all made up for you."

"That's very kind of you, Mrs. Rockwell." Amelia and Alice locked eyes for a moment.

Taking a deep breath and turning her gaze back towards her son, Alice again embraced Sam. "It's so nice to see you. Has Elijah visited you?"

"Just that one time during the war," Sam replied. "At this point I think it's safe to say he's ridden the elevator upstairs. But—"

"We'll see him again," Alice finished the sentence. "Yes, I know. I just wonder sometimes. Between the three of us, I'd prefer if Elijah Returned instead of Frank. But don't tell your father I said that."

Amelia gave Sam a wide-eyed look as they followed Alice inside. "That meeting with Elijah, that's when he Returned to tell you to become a detective, isn't it?"

"That's the one." Sam smiled at Amelia. "Worked out pretty well for me, I'd say." He set down his luggage while his mother hung up his hat and jacket. He looked for his father's ghostly form.

"Elijah always looked out for Samuel," Alice said, "Even when they were knee-high."

"Husband in another room?" Sam said to his mother. Alice stood with hands clasped, doting on her baby boy with a wide smile.

"Your father," said the widow, "disappeared sometime last night while I was sleeping. That happens sometimes, doesn't it?"

"I suppose so. There's a surprising amount of paperwork involved when you're sent back."

"Just listen to you." Alice hugged her son again. "You must have to learn quite a lot to be such a successful investigator."

Amelia caught Sam's eye and arched her eyebrow, forming a

wry smile.

Sam chewed on his lip, following his mother towards the living room. He faithfully wrote her, and might have overstated his pending success. That was only to keep her from worrying. Those letters were more like projections. The sort of thing his Father might send to a client, detailing what's coming in the next financial quarter.

"I think Sam and I are learning as we go," Amelia offered. "There's no real blue print for what your son is trying to achieve, but I think helping Returns is one of the noblest things a person can do with their life."

Alice beamed at Amelia's appraisal of her son. "Maybe you can write a book about what you learn."

"There's a lot to know, Mother." Sam shadowboxed as he walked. "Those boxing lessons taught me how to punch a fella in the nose real hard. That's useful."

"Oh, Samuel. Tell me you didn't get that shiner from fighting with some sort of gangster card shark."

"Nah, that was just a misunderstanding," Sam said, rubbing his cheek. "For murderers I mainly just swear and lob insults. It makes the criminal masterminds feel at home."

"Samuel!"

"He reads cheap detective books," Amelia said, amused at Alice's reaction. "He wants to copy what's inside. It's supposed to make him a better detective, but I think he'd be better off as himself." Sam gave a mock scowl at Amelia for leaking his secret.

Across the room, a wizened throat cleared itself. It was as disapproving a throat-clear as any Sam had heard. An elderly man with white hair and a square, bulldog jaw rose from his seat.

His pale blue eyes looked like they'd been diluted with water and he stared at Sam keenly through wire rimmed glasses. The hard look softened when the man's gaze turned to Amelia and Alice.

"This," Alice said in a tone Sam knew was meant to smooth over his faux pas, "is Reverend Silas Barnaby. I wrote you about him, Samuel. He was called to minister at our church this last February."

"Sorry about the cursing talk, Father."

"And call no man your father upon the earth," said Barnaby as he pointed an index finger skyward, "for one is your Father, which is in heaven. Thus sayest the Lord, and I'll not have the denigrations of the papacy about me, Mr. Rockwell, if you please."

Sam itched his cheek. "Mental lapse, Reverend." Sam gave a stunted and meager laugh. "In my line of work, it's the Priests who get most excited about Returns. They love a good exorcism." He rubbed the back of his neck when, expecting a laugh, he was given another austere look. "Reverend Barnaby, I'm here for my mother's sake. I'll need to ask her some questions. You're welcome to stay if it interests you."

"I'm here for your mother's sake as well, Mr. Rockwell," Barnaby interjected. "I'm here to provide succor and comfort."

"That's very kind of you," offered Amelia. She turned to Alice. "This must be so difficult for you."

Alice waved her hand.

"Death has parted she and her husband," Barnaby said, "and though Mrs. Rockwell wears not the ashen sackcloth of mourning, I have no doubt of her grief."

Amelia nodded earnestly, while Sam attempted to hide a sardonic grin behind his hand.

Ministers. Always so old fashioned. This one seemed like a relic from bygone Victorian days.

There were always those who treated death like some horrific tragedy, and it could be. A child loses his mother. Parents who lose a child. That sort of thing was awful. Knowing that people moved on tempered the grief, but rarely removed it altogether. But this case was different. Sam's parents spent a life together, over thirty years of marriage. They had a stable routine; things were provided for, and taken care of. Life would return to normal. Frank's death was more like an extended business trip. Everyone would see him again.

"Why don't we all sit down?" Alice suggested. Barnaby slid himself into a green armchair. Alice placed her hand on the Reverend's shoulder. "I'm fine. Really. We all die and then we all go on and everyone knows it. Frank left me well provided for. I was a little shaken up when I heard that Frank was murdered, I admit. But I'm sure that my Samuel will bring the killer to justice. That's the pressing concern now, making sure whoever did this doesn't harm anyone else." She walked half way into the kitchen and turned to Amelia, who was lingering, unsure whether to sit or remain standing like Sam. "Amelia, would you help me bring some coffee?"

From the lopsided frown on Barnaby's face, Sam could infer that he was not at all convinced by his mother's speech. Barnaby fixed his muted blue eyes on Sam, who took a seat near him. "Tell me, Mr. Rockwell. Samuel. Are you of similar contentment over your father's death?"

Several possible answers straight from the pages of I, the Jury sprang to Sam's mind. He didn't see the need to play the hard-boiled detective. Barnaby probably overheard Amelia giving up the tricks of his trade. The little stool pigeon.

"Well," Sam said, unconsciously rubbing the bump beneath his eye, "obviously I would have preferred that he live. But I agree with my mother. We've had plenty of time to get used to all of this life after death stuff. Why, it was back during the Civil War when the Returns really started showing up. Granted, not as many as during the fight against Hitler, but it's plain for all to see. Generations have been raised knowing without any doubt there's life after death. I say this generation is finally living like it. As a man of faith, I'd have thought you felt the same way. Aren't you keen on living for the next life?"

"And what of you?" Barnaby said, ignoring Sam's question. "Are you a man of faith?"

"Well, not professionally."

Barnaby seemed to struggle in holding a glower. He relinquished into a grin. "Samuel, my concern is not for the reality of the everlasting life hereafter. It is instead a concern for the way your mother, and you, I might add, are responding to your Father's death."

"Our response is fairly normal. I'm a bit surprised by yours. You're around the recently deceased as much as anyone. Short of the mortician, that is. I know the way Mother and I handle death isn't something you've never seen. Most people act the same as I do. Though there was this big Italian the other night..." Sam trailed off leaving only the sound of Alice and Amelia's chatting from the kitchen.

The Reverend harrumphed. "Most people do a number of things they'd be better off avoiding. Though the entire world may be of one accord, error remains error." The shadow of the Reverend's smile remained, and Sam felt much more at ease with the man.

Alice and Amelia came into the room to serve small, steaming teacups of black coffee. Barnaby nodded his thanks and blew gently into the delicate cup.

"Thanks," said Sam as the two women set their cups on the glass coffee table and sat together on a sofa opposite the men. "Well, Reverend," Sam said, winking at Amelia in the process, "You think you'll stick around for the investigation?"

"That reminds me," Alice said as she reached for a white business card resting on the coffee table. She handed the card to Sam, who stretched a long arm across the table to receive it. "Detective Clemons with the Tacoma Police Department said to call him at this number. I told him you'd be here before the lunch hour. He wants you to meet him at the crime scene."

A chime sounded from the Reverend's vest pocket. He removed a gold-chained watch. "I'm afraid I have another appointment to keep. I must deprive myself of your further hospitality, Mrs. Rockwell." He stood, the rest of the room also rising.

Alice led the Reverend to the door. "Thank you for coming."

Barnaby fitted a black derby hat over his stark white hair. "I do wonder," he said, "at the circumstances behind Mr. Rockwell's Return. Do you have much experience with why these people are permitted to come back?"

"It seems different every time," Amelia suggested, lifting her cup to her lips.

"The circumstances are wildly different," Sam shrugged. "But I think there are generally two reasons why folks Return."

The Reverend stood in the open door, interested.

"The first," Sam continued, "is to take care of some unfinished business. Maybe right a wrong."

"But not always," threw in Amelia. "Sometimes they just want to say goodbye."

"Or," resumed Sam, "let out some long buried secret."

"What's the second reason?" asked Alice.

Sam gave her a devilish grin. "To haunt someone for as long as they can. That old Dickens' story, A Christmas Carol? I hear it's the truth."

Alice went stiff. She softened quickly upon noticing Barnaby's inquiring look. She resumed the role of hostess with effortless grace. "Thank you again for identifying Frank's body this morning," she said to Barnaby. "I just couldn't stand the thought of seeing him like that."

"There's more to that statement than I think you realize, Alice." Barnaby said, straightening his jacket. "Comfortable as you might be with what comes after death, death itself is an aberration. Something that should not be, but is. All I ask of you, of you all, is to remember that."

"I think the same thing," Amelia nodded towards the reverend, her eyes earnest. Sam's eyes traced her face. She wasn't just being polite, he knew. With what happened to her parents, she believed every word. But then, she was young when her parents died, and that was one of the exceptions.

Reverend Barnaby tipped his hat in farewell and Alice closed the door behind him. Her body was rigid as she leaned against the closed door, her palms flat against the wood.

"I guess I'd better go meet this Detective Clemons," Sam said.

He saw his mother still at the door, frozen. "What's wrong?"

"Sam," she breathed, "Is it possible that Frank came back as... as... a haunt? He said they didn't tell him why he was sent back. But maybe, maybe he's going to haunt me and demand that I turn on his wrestling programs or drive him to visit his bowling friends until the day I die."

Sam shook his head. "Whatever the reason was, I'm sure it wasn't to haunt."

"How can you be sure?" asked Amelia.

"Because. He didn't show up at my place."

CHAPTER FIVE

Craftsmanship was creed. Sam repeated the advertising tag line with every smooth corner he turned. It had been his mother's idea for him to take Frank's Cadillac hardtop to meet Detective Clemons. His father would only use the car on nights and weekends, preferring to take public transportation and make more parking available to his customers. Even as an adult, Sam was never allowed to touch the car. Let alone drive it.

He reached Market Street and wished the ride could go longer. There was always the trip back to look forward to. Frank had driven Cadillacs as far back as Sam could remember. Now he knew why. This was something a fella could get used to. Maybe his father would leave the car to him. He'd ask him when he showed up again.

Spotting an open parking space in front of Rockwell Fiduciary, Sam pulled in behind a blue Packard. A trim man in brown flannel with a tan fedora leaned against the Packard, looking for signs of rain in newly formed summer clouds. The man peered at Sam through the Cadillac's windshield while he parked. Approaching the Cadillac, he waited on the curb while Sam exited the vehicle.

"Sam Rockwell?" the brown-suited man asked.

Sam nodded, and came around the front of the car to the stranger.

"Thought so. There's a family resemblance. I'm Detective Clemons."

It was time for Sam to get into character.

"Detective," Sam growled, shaking his hand. If Detective Clemons got an inkling that Sam didn't actually know what to do at a murder scene there would be no way he'd be able to work on the case. Family relations to the victim will only get a man so far.

The pair moved inside the building and passed a small crop of employees. The workers comforted one another, the shock of what happened to Frank still heavy.

"Well," said Sam, "What do you know so far?" He prepared himself. This was the part where the Detective would likely vet his credentials.

"We placed the murder sometime between five-thirty and five-forty five. The cause of death was a single gunshot to the back—pierced the heart—from a .38 Banker's Special. The weapon was found lying on the floor."

"That all?" Sam grunted, surprised at Clemons' willingness to go ahead. His act must be working.

"That's all so far."

They approached Frank's office. The door was guarded by the same blue-clothed officer who was assigned to tell Alice of her husband's death. Detective Clemons removed his hat, revealing a tuft of red hair. "Any sign?" Clemons asked Officer Dalton.

"No, Lieutenant."

The Detective bit his lip. "Where's your father, Detective Rockwell?"

"I haven't seen the deceased since I arrived," Sam said with indifference. Best not to use any terms of endearment. Project the cold and jaded detective, doing a favor for his mother. This is just another in a string of Return cases.

"I saw him last night," offered Dalton. "He seemed a short tempered fellow."

"Let's have that door open, Officer," Sam said, hoping he wasn't pushing it. Officer Dalton let the two detectives inside and resumed his watch.

The room was grand. Several times larger than Sam's closet in Los Angeles. Teakwood and ivory accented every corner. The brown molasses scent of rum and rich cigars still clung to the air, not quite overpowering the smell of blood. Large windows deluged the room with light, brightening considerably as the wind blew away the clouds.

Sam walked to his father's monolithic desk, the sound of footsteps completely absorbed by the lush carpet. Behind the desk, he could see his father's bloodstains as they dried in the sunlight. He squatted to examine a small open safe under the desk, bolted to the floor.

Empty.

Detective Clemons produced a handful of photographs taken the night before. "I was hoping your father could tell us what was in that safe. Do you have any ideas?"

Sam studied the photos intently. "No."

The photographs showed Frank slumped over his desk. Sam didn't need to be an actual detective to know he'd been seated and shot from behind. He had been flippant about his father's death. We all die and go on. Still, something about seeing his father's murdered body stirred sorrow in Sam's breast. He worked hard to keep the feeling from brimming over his eyes. Clemons seemed willing enough, but Sam couldn't blow his cover.

"Do you make it a habit to stand in the evidence?" Clemons asked through gritted teeth.

"Huh?" said Sam, second guessing his earlier assessment. Maybe Clemons wasn't so nice after all.

"Your shoes."

Sam looked at his feet. He stood in a dried puddle of his father's blood, a brown stain on the otherwise pristine carpet. He jumped back instinctively and hoped his face wasn't as red as it felt. Sam scrambled for something, anything, that would help him save face. "Uh," he managed, remembering at the last moment to use his working voice, "helps channel the dead. Maybe summon them. You said you wanted to talk to Frank, right?"

"Right," Clemons said with the slightest hint of a furrowed brow.

Great, thought Sam. He sounded more like a hoodoo psychic than a seasoned investigator. He needed to find something that would show Clemons he belonged on this case. He racked his mind for information about his father he might be able to make use of.

Frank always saw the last employee out the door at five. Overtime was forbidden for anyone but him. After locking up, he would check for any lights left on. With overhead costs under his control, he would retire to his office for a drink and any work that couldn't wait until the next day.

Sam rubbed his bruised cheek. His father would never have let a customer in after closing. Being late showed bad character. Whoever killed him was inside before the firm closed for the night. If Frank suspected he wasn't alone...

Sam ran his hand beneath his father's teak desk searching for the switch. He found it and pressed. A small hidden drawer opened with a pop.

"What's that?" Clemons demanded.

"My father kept a gun in here just in case anyone tried to hold the place up. Financial planners don't have any cash on site, but criminals aren't the brightest."

"Something wrong with your voice, Rockwell?"

In his excitement over where the gun led, Sam forgot to toughen is voice. "Drawer was closed," he said in sandpaper tones. "Either he didn't know someone was in the building with him or he knew his murderer personally. He would have grabbed his gun, otherwise."

Sam picked up a pearl-handled Colt m1911 pistol, hoping Clemons wouldn't pursue his changing voice further. The weapon felt cold in his hand. The gun was a gift from some happy investor from Fort Lewis. Sam was careful to keep his finger off the trigger. His father had taught him trigger discipline. His time in the Army reinforced it. Don't put your finger on the trigger unless you're ready to shoot.

"This was his," said Sam, this time remembering to speak the words with a growl. "I'll hold onto it." Taking the gun was probably against some sort of procedure.

"After we dust it for prints, other than yours I mean, detective."

Sam gulped and gingerly placed the weapon back in the open drawer. He would need to buy a shoulder holster first anyway. He rubbed his chin, eager to avoid a train wreck. "For Rockwell to be shot in the back he would need to have been comfortable enough to let the murderer come around behind him." Sam tossed the photographs onto his father's desk. "How about the employees? Any of 'em stay late last night?"

"I checked on all six," Clemons said with a shake of his head. He was opening up again, that was good. "Every one of them said it was a routine day. Turned out by five and home at the usual times. All of them have people ready to corroborate their alibis."

"Unless," Sam said shaking his finger at a newborn thought, "we have a conspiracy among the employees and their families."

"That a joke?" Clemons bristled.

Sam shrugged his shoulders. "I mean to say," he softened his growl, "that I've seen some strange things working Returns. How about the gun I see in this photo behind Frank's chair? That's the murder weapon. Any fingerprints?"

"Yes," Clemons confirmed. "We're checking to see if it matches anything we have on record."

"Huh," grunted Sam, "I would have expected the gun to be wiped clean seein' how it was left at the scene."

"Chalk it up to inexperience," suggested Clemons.

"Or surprise."

"Sure. What else can I help you with, detective?" Clemons said. There was a sort of mocking challenge to his words.

Sam ignored the Lieutenant and walked back to the office entrance, studying the carpet. It was muddled from too many trodden feet to be of much help. Only the corners of the room were still pristine from the last vacuuming, probably a few days ago. Sam stared at the far wall behind his Father's desk, a good twelve feet away. A painted portrait of Herbert Hoover hung above a veritable jungle of tall, green, potted plants.

Detective Clemons followed Sam's gaze. "Been a couple of presidents since then."

"He doesn't count the democrats, Hoover's up there until Eisenhower takes office. Not much chance of Ike losing."

Sam looked back to the far wall. His father swore by the effectiveness of the office's layout. He once told Sam that the room closed deals before he ever rose from his desk. The client's eyes would be drawn to the last "real" President and then his most faithful citizen servant, Frank Rockwell. Sam wasn't looking for someone to manage his investments. His focus was on the plants below the portrait.

When Sam was a boy, his mother would occasionally visit Frank in his office. While mother and father talked or ate lunch together, Sam and his brother Elijah pretended to hunt man-eating tigers in the thick greenery.

Pulling the window shades closed, the room grew dim from the sun's departure. Only a few yellow overhead lights kept the darkness at bay. Sam moved to the indoor forest, ducking down among the vegetation.

"Mind telling me what you're doing?" asked Clemons.

"How well can you see me, Lieutenant?" Sam shouted through

ferns.

"Not as well as you might think."

Sam sprang to his feet. "Right. And with only the desk lamp on?"

Detective Clemons caught on. "You think he was hiding in the bushes? We looked back there and didn't find anything."

"I think you missed something. Open the shades and then help me pull this plant out."

With an effort, Sam and Detective Clemons pulled the heavy pot across the floor. Sam pointed his forefinger at two round indentations on the otherwise smooth carpet.

"Looks like our trigger man was a woman," Sam said wryly. "These indentations come from a pair of ladies heels. I've been walked on by enough dames to recognize them on sight."

That last line was a little goofy. Even for a detective novel, thought Sam. He was pleased with actually uncovering a murder clue. Unless Clemons knew a reason to shoot the idea down.

"Could be from one of the gals watering the plants," Clemons said.

"No, he took care of these himself. Whoever shot him was hiding in the plant cover, I'm sure of it."

Clemons rubbed his chin vigorously, thinking the matter through when a burst of screams penetrated the office. Clemons pulled his weapon and rushed to the door. Officer Dalton greeted him with his weapon drawn as well. Sam stood dumbly for a moment then remembered Frank's pistol. He pulled the gun awkwardly from the drawer. By the time he caught up to Clemons and Dalton, the screams morphed into a crescendo of excited voices.

The employees, mourners moments before, were gathered in a circle taking turns to see who could talk the loudest. Four women splintered into a subgroup, speaking in excited whispers. A young man held the back of his head repeating, "Golly! Wow! Golly!"

In the middle of the circle stood Frank Rockwell. He waved his palms flatly at the ground as he sought to invoke some quiet. Sam and the police lowered their guns and looked to Frank expectantly.

"I've returned to save this proud nation from the destructive grip of the Soviet menace!" said Frank, squeezing his fist into a ball as if crushing an egg in his hand.

"Oh, good grief," Sam muttered to himself.

The girls began to volley questions about where Frank had been and what happened the night before. Sam could see that his father was beaming from the attention.

"There may be time for that tale later, my dears," said Frank. "But now more pressing matters await my expertise." He spotted Sam loitering in the hallway next to a police officer. "Ah! There's my boy!"

Frank walked to Sam, who grinned widely before becoming aware of his character's inconsistency. "Lieutenant Clemons," Sam said, sternly jumping back into his role, "This is Frank Rockwell, my father."

"Good," said Clemons. He stuck his hand out. "With a Return here, this case should be closed by tonight."

"I can't shake hands any longer," Frank said. "You wouldn't enjoy it if I tried. What do you mean closed by tonight? You haven't found my murderer yet?"

"Your son may have found us a solid piece of evidence, but I was hopeful you might help fill in the gaps," answered Clemons. "Did you see the shooter?"

"No, of course not. One must take Frank Rockwell by surprise or not at all." Frank shook his head. "I didn't see him."

"Her," corrected Sam.

"Don't be foolish, Samuel," Frank chided.

Sam stifled an eye roll. Detective Slade Hammer never encountered his own father in the pulp fiction pages.

"Can you tell me anything out of the ordinary about last night?" asked Clemons.

"My wife failed to make pot roast."

Detective Clemons dropped his pencil and notebook to his side. "Anything about the time before or after you were shot?"

"No."

"And here I thought talking to the victim would make for an easy case," Clemons sighed.

"Are you sure you can't think of anything?" Sam asked. "The more help you can give now, the sooner you can get back home to spend however much time you've got left with mother."

"I can tell you why I was murdered, and why I'm back," Frank said. He spoke with self-importance and cleared his throat for effect. "Atomic. Secrets."

Frank savored the surrounding reactions. His employees were in awe. Officer Dalton looked troubled. Clemons looked contemplative and Sam looked lost.

"I oversee the investments for a number of the mathematicians and scientists who worked on the Manhattan Project," Frank declared with no small amount of pride. "One of them, I won't reveal who, gave me a dossier with government secrets about an atomic weapon nearly one hundred times as powerful as anything currently in existence. I kept the file in my office safe." Frank mustered all the gravity he was able and concluded dolefully, "Were that information to fall into Soviet hands, all would be lost for our great nation."

There was a somber silence. At length Sam broke the spell and addressed the small crowd of Rockwell Fiduciary employees. "Did any of you—" he stopped short and deepened his voice. "Did any of you see a woman come in sometime just before closing yesterday?"

"Samuel what are you after? A date? No woman shot Frank Rockwell." To Frank's alarm, two of his secretaries raised their hands.

"I saw a woman with short brown hair and a black tweed chenille dress come in not long before closing," said a woman with cat eye glasses, a pencil sticking from her hair bun.

"Good," said Sam, "anything else?"

"She was with Charlie Cox, but I didn't see them leave together," said the other woman.

"Where's Cox?" yelled Frank.

"I let him head back to his apartment earlier," said Clemons. "His neighbors backed up his alibi and he said being at the scene of a crime made his stomach turn."

Looks like I need to see if this Cox fellow wants to be my new friend, thought Sam. It was a good line. He opened his mouth to deliver it when Frank blurted, "Let's go find out what Charles knows. Come along, Samuel."

A couple of the girls tittered. Sam frowned. Partly because

of the laughter but also because the best retort he could think of was, Sure, you could use someone to watch your back. He couldn't bring himself to cut down his own father. "Be right with you," Sam said roughly,

"Fine," said Clemons, "but wait a moment. Mr. Rockwell, what you've said brings up a whole set of complications. This case is going to go to the FBI. I'll need you to remain available for further questioning."

"No finer men than Hoover's boys," said Frank. "I'll be with Samuel, or else at my private residence."

"I guess there's no use trying to detain a spook. Sam, can I talk to you a moment before you go?"

Sam and Clemons stepped outside while Frank turned his attention back to his employees.

"Is your father telling me the truth?" Clemons asked.

"He's got a flair for theatrics." The father's flair was showing itself in Sam's caricature of a detective. Clemons was willing to let him interview Cox. The act seemed to be working. "I think he's telling you the truth, though. If he gave you a reason different than what he told 'em upstairs he'd be recalled again."

"Recalled again?"

"Last night he disappeared from his bed, he's not the type to take a midnight stroll. I wasn't sure he'd be back at all until now."

The detective tilted his head and gave a half puckered frown. "Why stand in the blood, then?"

Sam's insides jumped. He issued a toothy smile. "Oh, just doing what I can."

Clemons eyeballed Sam and nodded. "They wouldn't send him back here a second time if he wasn't telling the truth, I suppose."

"It's unlikely, but not impossible. They aren't Santa Claus, they don't see everything. It's angels mainly, but like us they can make a mistake."

Sam began to make his way back inside the building when Clemons tugged on his jacket. The detective looked furtively from side to side. "So is the place like Purgatory?"

Sam shook his head. "Never heard it described like that. More like a big city hall. Most folks do some paperwork and pass through. Some request to be sent back and others are sent back without having to ask."

"This all started after the first battle of Bull Run, right? I got work to do, but you're the expert. What can you tell me that will help me in the future?"

Sam's stomach jumped at being called an expert. He was the only person he knew of who tried to make working with Returns a career. A career that wasn't exactly going swimmingly. He didn't really have any special knowledge you couldn't read in a book somewhere. But Clemons seemed interested. Maybe Sam could use that interest to solidify his involvement on the case.

"I think it's been going on longer than that," Sam replied. "I met a Return who swore that Macbeth was a true story. Said he saw Lord Banquo sitting on a bench wearing a kilt."

Clemons straightened up and walked a semicircle around Sam. "Don't try and goof with me, Sam."

Sam held out his hands plaintively. "It's what I heard." He snapped his fingers, picking up where he left off. "Why are we seeing so many more of these Returns now? I can't say. The war? The bomb? Just became the right time? You'd best talk to a Minister for that answer. I met a swell Presbyterian this morning."

Clemons chuckled. "My wife and Father Donaldson would both kill me for converting."

Sam gave a full hearted laugh. He felt comfortable with Clemons and it was causing him to let down his guard and cut the act. He didn't actually know the Detective very well, so Sam decided to push on with the gumshoe subterfuge.

"Listen," said Sam as he patted his keys, "if heaven sent Frank Rockwell down because some Soviet female super spy is set to blow up the USA, we'll have to move decisively." The detective nodded intently at Sam, but said nothing. Sam pressed on, his voice almost rasping from the edge he threw into it. "There are certain procedures and lines that you and Officer Dalton back there have to follow. I, on the other hand—"

"Stop talking," Detective Clemons said shortly.

Sam was busted. He pushed the hardnosed, play by your own rules act and it wasn't going to fly.

"Go and visit Cox," Clemons said, "but don't tell me anything further. You have my number. Keep me informed. But only tell me what I need to hear about the case."

Sam gave a relief-fueled smile and clapped Clemons on his arm.

"You're a real choice guy, Detective," Sam said, not entirely sure he meant it. Was Clemons willing to let him beat up a suspect or hold Cox over the edge of a roof like in the novels?

The Lieutenant drove away in his blue Packard while Sam made his way around the front of the Cadillac. He caressed the hood with a single smooth motion of his hand and pulled the keys from his slacks.

"STOP!" A voice pierced the air and silenced the jingle of keys. Frank waved his arms frantically, as if to ward off an errant fighter plane seeking to land on an aircraft carrier.

"Stop!" he yelled again. "Do not touch my car, Samuel! H-how did you find the keys? Who-o said you could touch my baby? This is my car, Samuel! No one drives her but, but Papa Frank!"

Sam stood with a bemused smile. He rested both arms on the roof of the car, which seemed to aggravate his father further. "Mother gave me the keys, Papa Frank," Sam let loose a chuckle. "You can have them back if that's what you want."

He tossed the keys at Frank. Once a receiver at Yale, Frank raised a hand to pull in the flying metal as it soared through the air. He missed completely. The keys passed through hands, arms, and body, finally landing with a krish on the concrete sidewalk, glinting in the afternoon sun.

Frank stomped alternating feet like a majorette leading a high school marching band. "Fine," he sighed. "You may drive her. But not without me." He walked to the car and, remembering his ethereal state, passed through the door to sit in the passenger seat.

Sam jogged to pick up the keys, returned, and ducked inside the car. He ignited the engine and adjusted the mirror. "Where does Cox live?"

"Why would I know that?"

Sam sighed, exited the vehicle and jogged back inside the building. A vivacious brunette gave him the address from Cox's employee file. Sam considered practicing his tough guy lothario routine on the woman, but remembered how Miss Bouvier reacted in his office and thought better of it.

Frank was staring a hole into the Cadillac's dash when Sam returned. "Flick off that piece of dust, would you son?"

Sam obliged and put the car in gear.

"Easy now," said Frank. "Let her idle for a few moments. That's fine. There's the turn signal. Good. Ease her out, Son— watch for that black Desoto!"

"Father, I know how to drive fine," said Sam. "I got the car here without any dents or scratches."

"I know," Frank said, "I checked while you were inside."

"I'm a whole lot more likely to put a ding in your baby with you jabbering at me the whole trip."

The Cadillac left for Charles Cox's apartment building with Frank doing his best to keep silent. He did admirably, only throwing his hands up in alarm every other turn and shouting a warning once when a grocery truck seemed too close to his black beauty.

Sam grew accustomed to his father's ejaculations after a mile or so. The weight of what he, Sam Rockwell, was investigating came down on him like a pneumatic press. What in the wide blue world was he doing looking into atomic secrets? Why did his father have them in the first place? Sam considered turning the car around and telling Detective Clemons the truth— that most of his "experience" came from the pages of comic books and pulp fiction. That would be a swell conversation.

He ran over the possible scenario.

"My last case involved staking out a lonely housewife to find evidence of adultery, and then being punched out by her husky husband. Clearly I'm qualified to assist in a murder investigation involving doomsday weapons."

Even if he did come clean to Clemons, what then? Get arrested? Admit to his parents that the extent of his work was as a glorified message boy for the occasional spook who found his office?

No. He would make it work or die trying. He hadn't thought of that before.

The dying.

He could actually die, the same as his father, if he wasn't careful. Sam patted the gun beneath his jacket. He should probably ask his father if he could keep it. With how Frank reacted to him driving the car, he wasn't so sure he'd agree. His father didn't seem keen about moving into the hereafter.

"Let up on the gas, Samuel!" Frank chided in a roar. "You'll give the engine a knock."

"Sorry," Sam said absentmindedly. He slowed down, already at his destination; the Puget Villa apartment building. An open space waited for them, right up front. A perk of driving while the rest of the city was still at work.

"Maybe you should stay inside," said Sam.

Frank stepped through the door to the surprised yelp of a pedestrian who observed the unusual disembarkment. "What for?" he said. "It's not like I can be murdered again. Besides, I know Charles. He worships the ground I walk on. He'll be a help."

"Maybe," said Sam. He added a rough edge to his voice to get back into character. "But lemme do the talking. And stay hidden at first, all right, Pops? Just in case he isn't squeaky clean as you believe. They never are."

"Why are you talking like that, Samuel?"

"Oh," said Sam his voice modulating to normal. "Just playing the character. Folks read the crime and detective novels and expect a P.I. to eat nails and tell it like it is. So I make sure to give them what they want. I figure it'll help with growing the business."

"Is it working?"

"So far it isn't hurting. Besides, I learned it from the Rockwell school of business."

"When I told you to meet your customers' expectation I didn't expect you to go around speaking like Humphrey Bogart with a sore throat."

Sam shrugged and climbed the building's front steps. A brass trimmed directory listed names behind a plate of glass.

C. Cox. Apt 32-C.

Sam buzzed the corresponding button and turned to his father. "Just follow my lead, okay?"

Frank raised a finger to protest but fell silent when a voice squawked from the metal box.

"Yeah?" buzzed the voice.

"Charles Cox?" Sam asked.

"Yeah?"

"I've got some more questions about Frank Rockwell's murder."

"Detective Clemons?"

"No, Detective Spade," Sam said.

Frank shook his head. There was a pause.

"C'mon up."

CHAPTER SIX

The front doors buzzed, allowing Sam to pull them apart. He held one door open for his father. Realizing this was unnecessary, he let the door shut on Frank while he was only halfway inside. Frank threw up his hands to guard his face from the heavy doors, but they passed through him entirely.

Sam laughed.

Frank rolled his eyes. "Very funny, Detective Spade. Whoever that is."

"Maltese Falcon," said Sam as he bounded up the stairs. His long legs propelled him at a speed Frank couldn't match. He yelled down over his shoulder, "Good book!"

Frank shook his head and attempted to catch up by taking two stairs at a time. He tripped over his own feet on the second flight, but instead of falling face first into the blue carpeted stair, floated upward, gliding to the top of the second landing.

"Wonderful," said Frank, "I'm now a card carrying member of the freak show."

He continued floating up the steps, planting his feet once he reached the third floor. He walked to Sam, who gestured for him to hurry up.

The men stood on either side of the door to Cox's apartment. 32-C.

"He might be armed," whispered Sam.

Frank rolled his eyes. "Well are you? I hope so, for your mother's sake."

Holding open his jacket to reveal his new pistol, tucked in his waistband, Sam winked at his father. "Can I have this?"

"Oh, so it's time to divide your father's earthly possessions, is it?" Frank said, too loud for stealth.

"Shhh!" Sam held his finger against his lips and reached out to clamp a hushing hand to his father's mouth. Remembering his father's condition, Sam pulled back his hand before it could be chilled by Frank's spectral cold. The close call gave him an idea.

"Stick your ghostly head through the wall there and see if he's got anything or anyone in there with him," Sam ordered.

Frank paused to grimace at Sam and then pushed his face through the wall. It quickly popped back out. "I think he's gone!" Frank whispered. "It's pitch black inside."

"Gone? Unless he took the fire escape we would have seen him come out the front door and down the stairs."

Frank looked again, longer this time. He returned with a sheepish smile. "There's a closet on the other side of this wall."

"That explains the dark," said Sam. "Try looking through the door. Carefully."

Frank stood before the apartment's front door and slowly moved his left eye toward the peephole. Eye and cheek passed through and scanned the room. He withdrew his face and turned to Sam. "He's on his sofa and looks upset. Probably over my death. He has his head in his hands. I didn't see a gun."

"Okay," Sam said in a hushed tone, "I'm going to knock on the door. Hide somewhere down the hall so he doesn't see you when he opens it."

Frank acquiesced while Sam got back into character. He knocked on the door.

"Charles Cox? I'm the detective you buzzed in."

Muffled footfalls shuffled to the door, which swung open to reveal a young man with dark, greased hair and pale complexion. Cox wore his black work trousers, but had removed his shirt and tie, wearing only a white v-neck undershirt. He bid Sam enter and closed the door behind him.

Frank quickly tiptoed to the door and walked through the wall and into the closet to better hear the interview.

The apartment was modestly furnished with chrome legged vinyl furniture the color of split pea soup. Cox waved a hand at an empty chair and collapsed back onto the sofa.

"I'll stand," Sam said flatly. He removed a pencil and small bound notepad from his coat pocket. Cox didn't seem dangerous, and hadn't asked Sam for any identification. So far, so good. "Let me have your alibi again. I wanna have my own record," Sam ordered. "Start with your name and occupation.

Cox squinted at the private investigator. "Charles Cox. Is it necessary to repeat all of this again? I told Detective Clemons everything I knew."

"Nobody but Clemons can make sense of his chicken scratch and I wasn't there when Clemons interviewed you. That's not a problem is it?"

Perhaps it was a bit soon to flex any muscle, but it was better to take control early. Sam felt he'd done a good job in crafting his answer. He didn't actually come out and say he was a member of the local police. He just let Cox think it.

"Charles Cox. I work at Rockwell Fiduciary..."

The closet darkness was tedious to Frank. It made him think of his body, probably in a coffin somewhere. He shuddered. With no desire to stand among old blankets and coats just listening, Frank ventured his head through the closet door. To his right was the front door, a hall leading to the living room was on his left. Frank could see Cox's feet gently kicking a coffee table in front of where he sat. Sam stood taking notes, his back to Frank. Neither of the two men noticed his head poking through the closed door.

Retreating back to the darkness, Frank slowly walked through the back of the closet. It took longer than he expected. This apartment must have thick walls.

Light soon greeted Frank from a small bathroom. A claw-foot tub ringed with a white shower curtain sat before him. Last night's damp towels still draped over its side. From the corner of his eyes, Frank found that his head was still half inside a mirrored medicine cabinet. His legs stood inside the toilet. Frank was thankful that he couldn't feel cold or dampness.

"Good night," Frank sighed to himself, relieved that no one was making use of the facilities at his arrival. He clucked at the untidy clumps of clothing strewn about the green tiled floor.

With no desire to return to the closet, Frank looked out the ajar bathroom door. Satisfied that no one was watching, He decided to use his newfound ability to float out of the bathroom.

Arriving in a small hallway branching from the main entrance hall, Frank touched down silently. A linen cabinet anchored the end of the hall. Through an open door Frank saw an absolute sty of a bedroom, so messy that even hogs would straighten things up a bit before laying down.

Frank kept his disapproval silent, resisting the urge to cluck his tongue again.

He stole into the bedroom, obeying a curiosity about the home life of one of his employees. As in the bathroom, clothing littered the floor. The drawers and closets looked like ground zero over Tornadoville, Kansas. The bed was unmade and Cox evidently took his breakfast in his room.

Frank shook his head at three days' worth of partially consumed toast and eggs on red dinner plates crowded atop a dresser. Two empty glasses of orange juice rested on a nightstand. A third glass stained with red lipstick had tipped over on the opposite nightstand, its sticky contents absorbed by the carpet.

Frank raised his eyebrows at this newly uncovered scandal. Cox wasn't a married man. He heard his name spoken from the living room and moved into the hall to better hear.

"Frank Rockwell?" It was Samuel seeking some sort of clarification. The disdain in Sam's voice drove the evidence of an apparent tryst the night before from Frank's mind. What jumped down his pants? Part of an act or no, Frank felt he deserved better treatment than Sam's tone afforded him. He was a murder victim for Pete's sake. His interest aroused, Frank crept closer to the room holding Cox and Samuel.

"Sure," Cox said in answer to Sam. "My neighbors are very kind, just like Mr. Rockwell."

"Huh," said Sam, scribbling in his notepad.

"They feed me a nice meal every Wednesday night," Cox continued. "I came straight here and had dinner with them. Mister Carver and his wife are probably home next door if you want to ask them for your notebook, but Detective Clemons already sent someone to talk with them."

Cox drifted into a forlorn grimace. "It's strange to think I was one of the last faces Mr. Rockwell ever laid eyes on."

Still hidden in the hall, Frank put his hand to his heart and bowed his head. Finally, some gratitude. Someone was behaving in a manner fitting of his magnanimous person-hood.

"That seems an uncommon affection for Mr. Rockwell," Sam said.

"Oh, no," Cox said, tears welling in his eyes. "We all thought the world of him. He was firm, but the finest man of business I ever met. He paid us fairly and was quick with a word of advice or encouragement if we ever needed it. So long as it was professional in nature."

Frank rejoiced silently in the hall.

"Keep it together," Sam said shortly. "We're almost done and then you can curl up and have a good cry over dear old Frank Rockwell."

Cox straightened himself and abashedly used his wrists to push the tears from his face.

"Your co-workers reported having seen a woman at your desk shortly before closing. Tell me about her."

"A woman?" Cox asked with a sniff. "Do you think she shot Mr. Rockwell?"

Sam's eyes narrowed. "I don't think anything. So why don't you tell me?"

Cox opened his mouth to answer, but instead issued a noise that ranged between a cough and a sob. His eyes darted swiftly about the room.

Sam sensed a sudden panic seeping from the man's pores. He hardened his gaze while the other man smoothed down his hair. Cox put a fist to his mouth and squeezed tears through his tightly closed eyes.

"I'm sorry," he shuddered, "I just can't help thinking about poor Mr. Rockwell."

"Look," said Sam in a half shout. "I need to talk with whoever this woman is. She was in the office close enough to the end of the day to be a person of interest. Now she went straight to you and didn't talk to anyone else when she came into the joint. Who is she?"

"There, there, Charles!" Frank loudly soothed his new favorite employee as he entered the room.

Cox let out a terrified scream and kicked the coffee table over in his distress. Sam jumped back to avoid the tumbling magazines and ash tray. Cox looked to his ghostly employer with wide and fearful eyes.

Frank was somewhat perturbed at this reaction but softened again. "I want to thank you for your fitting words of kindness," he said.

The frightened gaze remained in Cox's eyes. Swallowing hard he nodded his head swiftly in an acceptance of Frank's gratitude.

"Mr. Rockwell," Sam said "has been sent back." He drew his notepad to chest height and said, "We can both be out of your place if you play ball and tell me where to find the girl."

"I-I barely know her," Cox stammered. "We'd only recently met. I told her to speak with me if she was ever interested in investing some money that had been left to her."

"What's her name?" asked Sam.

"Gayle..." Cox trailed off. "Gayle something. Or other. I don't know. That's all I know."

Sam saw something in the abruptness of Cox's answer. A fog of suspicions gathered in his mind. Now was the time that any leather necked detective would press Cox more severely. Twist his arm and see about rattling the man into admitting more than he let on.

"You know where you met her," spat Sam, instantly proud of his delivery.

"Oh... sure," Cox sputtered.

Frank's eyes bulged in surprise. Cox cast a pleading glance for his boss to intercede.

"Don't look at him, look at me!" yelled Sam. "You don't want to talk about her any further? Is that it? Why. Tell me! Where did you meet her?"

"I can't say."

"You will say!" Sam gathered to his full height. He clenched his fists, towering over Cox. The smaller man shrunk back into the sofa, anticipating the pending blows of Sam's fist.

"Control yourself, Samuel," said Frank, putting his ghostly form between Sam and Cox, his legs hidden within the overturned furniture, "or I'll report you to the police. Even if you are my son."

A river of discernment and relief washed over Cox's face. He left the protective burrow of his sofa and stood, slow and deliberate. A smirk briefly touched his face. "You led me to believe you were with the police."

Sam swallowed hard. Visions of his arrest danced before him like demons around a bonfire. Impersonating an officer and threatening bodily harm. That would go over real well with Clemons. He looked to his father in dismay. His first big case and "Papa Frank" blows his cover.

Frank paid his son no mind. He turned to Cox and spoke to him softly, as if comforting a frightened child. "I was murdered because I had in my possession a dossier of atomic secrets," he said. "Such information could give the communists a permanent advantage over our brave republic. Where did you meet this girl, Charles? You can tell me."

Cox itched his nose. After a long pause he said, "A bar called The Working Man."

Frank nodded appreciatively. "Ah. So a bar is the big secret you can't part with?" he said. "Nothing to be ashamed of. I enjoy a nice drink now and again myself."

Cox was all smiles. He stared directly into Sam's eyes, challenging him. "I guess I'm old fashioned."

"Good, good," said Frank, giving the man a paternal smile. He beamed from solving this most elusive of mysteries. "Like I said, no shame at all in having a little drink every now and again." He turned to Sam. "Let's leave Mr. Cox to clean up."

Frank walked down the hall and through the front door.

Cox arched both eyebrows and gave Sam a half smile. Sam set his jaw and left the apartment with swift, pounding steps.

The evening sun was pink and gold. Summer in the northwest. Sam exited the Puget Villa apartment building without noticing. Frank, already outside, stood with the additional height that comes to a man after an unequivocal success. With hands on hips Frank admired the setting sun's vivid reflection as it radiated off the shining chrome of his great automotive pride. Like a king surveying a treasury of glittering gold, Frank fawned over his Cadillac.

"I'd say I cracked the case," said Frank. "Through sheer strength of character. Hopefully you took good notes on that pad of yours."

"Sure, swell ones," Sam kept his voice hard and in character. He waved a fist menacingly. "Why'd you have to blow my cover like that? Don't make me get rough, old man."

"There you go with that voice again." Frank stuck out his chin and winked. "Let me have it, son."

Sam buried his hands in his pant pockets. Even if he actually wanted to, all that would happen would be a bone dampening swipe through spectral mist.

Frank nodded and said, "This act of yours is getting carried away, Samuel. You might have beaten poor Charles to death if I hadn't intervened."

"Ah, I wasn't going to rough him up, just make him think so. I still think he's better acquainted with that dame—woman," Sam corrected himself. "Sorry, Pop. More than he lets on."

"I'm sure Charles told us everything he knows. He met her on a single occasion at a tavern and offered her an opportunity to improve her life through fiscal planning and responsibility. You have yet to thank me for discovering that vital piece of information, son."

"Thanks. It is a good lead. Still, I'm fairly certain old Charles was offering Gayle a whole lot more than financial advice."

"Silly." Frank shook his head, feeling obligated to cover up his employee's immoral indiscretions. "Now drive me home."

"We've got to get to that tavern," Sam said as he opened the car door. "Float on in."

"What? Not at all. Didn't you hear what Charles had to say about me? I need to go straight home and tell your mother. That should change her attitude."

"What attitude?"

"Your mother is not mourning me as she should."

"Oh, so?"

Frank jabbed his index finger at the pink and golden sky. "Lamentations! Weeping! That's the sort of emotional outpouring that should accompany Frank Rockwell's departure from this world."

"Like Mary & Martha over Lazarus?"

"Sure," said Frank, lowering his hand. "Probably."

"You haven't really gone anywhere since you were knocked off." Sam shrugged. The fact of it was, Sam knew his parents weren't all that close. They loved each other, sure. But both put their time and passion into things other than their marriage. Frank's constant focus was his business while Alice had occupied herself with the raising of her two sons, then actively supporting missionaries when Sam and Elijah reached adulthood.

"What's that supposed to mean?"

Sam adjusted his tie and looked his father in eye, smiling. "You know the saying, 'Gone, but not forgotten?' Well, you're here and not forgotten. And even if you were gone, the fact that you weren't sent on a freight elevator straight down means that we'll see you again before too long. I was telling your Pastor—"

"Her Pastor. He tries to tell me what I can and can't do too much."

"Alright, her Pastor. I was telling Reverend Barnaby that death really has lost its sting now that the curtain's been drawn back and everyone and their uncle can see the step that comes after that last breath."

"Unless the next breath is full of fire and brimstone."

"Well, Father," Sam smiled, "some people don't like being told what to do."

Lieutenant Clemons' blue car pulled up and squeaked its brakes. The detective leaned out of the driver side window. "Thought I'd see if the two of you if you were still here," he said. "Find anything out?"

"Possibly," Sam said, a hint of steel now in his voice. "Pretty sure the dame in question saw Cox, who says she can sometimes be found at a place called The Working Man."

"I know that place," said Clemons. "When I was still a beat Cop I was called out there more than once for drunk and disorderlies. The place has a building-clearing brawl at least once a quarter."

"Sounds lovely," Sam growled.

"Did Cox frequent that hole?" asked the Detective. "It's not exactly a sophisticated sort of establishment."

Sam shot his father an I-told-you-so smirk.

Frank grimaced and looked down at his car. "You're certainly not taking my baby anywhere near a place like that," he said, passing into his Cadillac with only his head sticking outside. "I have half a mind to march back upstairs and reprimand Cox for his choice in restorative locales. Drive me home, Samuel."

"Sorry Pop, no time for that. This lead is as hot as it's going to get. I have to get over there before your employee of the month gets cold feet and warns his sugar-girl of what's coming."

Frank wore his irritation like a wool undershirt, but refrained from blowing his son's cover again. "Take me home, son."

Sam shook his head.

Detective Clemons, seeing the disagreement, piped in. "The Working Man is within walking distance, just down on the waterfront. I can drive you home, Mr. Rockwell. I need to know exactly where to find you once my FBI contact calls back."

"Oh, alright," said Frank. "Sam, pick my car up on your way back home."

The method-acting detective waved in acknowledgment, already several paces down the sidewalk.

A saline breeze refreshed Sam as he reached the promenade. Darkness descended from the gathering night sky, repelled by the electric hum of the city street lights. Sam tipped his hat at an oncoming couple walking arm-in-arm, then placed it in the crook of his arm to join his jacket. Fifteen minutes of strenuously fast walking made the warm summer's eve feel oppressively hot.

Commencement Bay rippled gently, the lapping water blending with excited teenagers sharing milkshakes in a nearby malt shop. The familiar sounds caused Sam to think of his brother, Elijah. As children, the brothers visited ice cream parlors and malt shops whenever a little tin could be found in their pockets. That meant often, given their mother's doting.

Later in life, as co-owners of a restored 1932 Chevy 6, Sam would drive dates to the malt shop he now walked by. Invariably, Elijah would get a friend to take him early to stake out an adjoining booth. The older brother would eavesdrop, offering Sam advice that varied wildly from sage to foolish at the end of the night.

"Did Darlene give you a kiss goodnight?" Elijah once said after Sam returned from a highly anticipated date.

"None of your business, jelly bean."

"Three strikes and you're out. The trick is this—and trust me, I know from experience—at the end of the night, when you're with her on her mother's porch, you've got to take her softly by the hands and rub them gently with your thumbs, like this." Elijah took Sam by the hands and stared longingly into his eyes.

"Cut it out!" Sam tried to pull away, but his older brother's grip was too strong.

"No! This really works. Look deep into her eyes, just like this, and say, 'Darlene, you have the face of an angel. Your beauty takes my breath away, and if I don't tell you something right now, I'll regret it until the end of my days.'"

"So what do you say then?" Sam asked.

Elijah winked, leaned in as if to whisper the secret to a woman's heart, and let out a tooth-shuddering belch into Sam's ear. He howled hysterically as Sam's facade of anger melted into a snickering laugh. Elijah's deep belly laughs then grew frantic, waking both parents.

A wistful smile brushed Sam's face. He missed his brother. Peering as he walked by the malt shop's large plate glass window; he sought further memories like old friends.

Inside, a teenage boy leaned against the counter and conjured some reason to caress his date's dark curls. The girl's face turned crimson. Sam imagined him and Amelia doing the same. His stomach rode a roller coaster while visions of his erstwhile secretary set his heart dancing. Sam took two swift steps, starting a foxtrot, before shaking the image from his head.

He glanced around and felt relief that no one had seen him. Flatfoot gumshoes kept their hearts closed off from the outside world, and here he was nearly dancing around like Fred Astaire. Sam needed to get back into character.

Cresting a hill, he saw The Working Man appear. A faint din of voices and laughter issued forth from the dimly lit cedar building. Trouble was coming. He could sense it. He really needed to get into character. Sam Rockwell doesn't mind a reasonable amount of trouble, he thought to himself.

Pushing his hat forward onto his head, Sam readied himself to find his father's killer.

The Working Man tavern overlooked the water at the end of an old wooden pier that branched off from the concrete promenade. A halo of smoke issued from windows tilted half open into the night air. The smoke raised to wreath a track of hooded overhead lamps, weakly shining on silvered cedar shingles.

Two men sat on the thick cords of rope that served as a guard rail along the pier. They took no notice of Sam, their eyes instead peering into the shallow green that lapped beneath them. The men's dungarees and filth-crusted fingernails indicated to Sam that The Working Man's patrons were a reflection of its namesake.

Inside, thick calloused hands gripped mugs, bottles, and shot glasses. The scent of stale alcohol and dried sweat followed the Longshoremen as they mingled with drivers, sailors, teamsters, and mill workers. A thin man leaned against a wooden support beam, habitually adjusting his brown tie and drawing designs on one of the few girls present.

Sam expected to be the only man wearing a suit in the joint and thought the regulars might give him some trouble for it. Tacoma was a blue collar town with blue collar rules. But none of the burly men, many still wearing their varied uniforms, seemed to mind him. Only the thin man cast anything more than a fleeting glance in his direction.

"Scotch, rocks," Sam said to the bartender, a greasy fellow with a gray beard and barren scalp. Scotch on the rocks was a drink you could easily pretend to consume, just sip until the melting ice dilutes the liquor's color. The barkeep delivered a glass containing such dingy ice that Sam was sure it was made from the Bay's water below. A shadow loomed over the drink. Sam looked up to see the barkeeper staring at him expectantly.

"That'll do for now," said Sam. "I'll ring the bell if I need you again."

The bearded proprietor grunted and headed further down the bar. Excellent form, Rockwell. Hammett couldn't have written it better.

Glass clunked on wood, notifying Sam that someone had sidled up next to him. Sam looked casually over his shoulder and saw the thin man, who wore a not-quite drunk smile on his rosy face. The man propped his head up with his fist and smiled.

"Are you sympathetic?" asked the Thin Man. His voice was high with a hint of nasal.

"Not if they have it coming."

The thin man adjusted his tie. "Just stopping in then."

"Sounds about right," said Sam. The dirty ice began to melt in his drink. "A fella told me about the place earlier today, said he picked up a dame or two. Thought I'd come by while I was in town."

"I might know your friend. I'm something of a regular here." The thin man's slender fingers readjusted his tie. "I may not look it, but I fit in nicely with working class."

Sam shrugged indifferently. "You know Charles Cox?"

"Interesting." The thin man's words traveled almost entirely through his nose. "I have in fact seen Mr. Cox here from time to time." He gestured to a corner booth. "Why don't we take a seat and discuss our mutual friend? My name is Leonard, by the way." Leonard the thin man offered his hand.

The two shook. "Call me Sam." He followed Leonard to a round, corner booth in the rear of the building.

"Don't forget your drink."

"I didn't," Sam said, leaving the glass on the counter. Green vinyl, darkened by the unwashed grime of countless hands, creaked as Sam took a seat opposite the thin man. "The only drink I like dirty is a martini," said Sam. He was in rare form.

Leonard tugged on a shirt sleeve. "How long have you known Charles Cox?"

"I don't know him all that well. Met him through one of his co-workers. He said he met a nice girl here and I thought I'd see how well the store was stocked."

"You might find some share croppers here," Leonard said absently. He removed a stray string wrapped around a button, never meeting Sam's eyes. An index finger waggled, and Sam tensed as a towering man, wide as a city bus, emerged from the den of drinkers. The hulking man approached the table and sat, sandwiching Sam between himself and the thin man.

Tall as Sam was, he had to look up to the blond, flat-topped bull. "Who are you? Donald Duck?"

"This is my friend, Dimitry." Leonard said. He blew a stubborn piece of fuzz from his jacket. "I think he would very much like to know the name of the girl Charles met here."

Sam brushed his arm against his father's pistol. He still had it. Maybe Dimitry joined for fun and fellowship, but the spider of bad feelings was spinning a web for Sam. It seemed to him just as likely that the two men knew something about the murder. He decided to stay in character.

"So go ask Cox," said Sam.

"Cox is no here," Dimitry said with a deep Soviet accent.

"What's her name?" Leonard repeated.

"I don't remember. Why don't we just say it was Lauren Bacall and be done with it? I only came to see if there was a nice girl I could meet and enjoy a night out with."

The alcoholic rosiness left Leonard's face, replaced by a cold disaffection. "Who are you really looking for, Mister—" he cut his nasal snarl short, "Sam?"

Sam feigned puzzlement. "A nice girl, like I said. I saw you talking to one pretty enough when I first came in."

"You don't know her like I do," squeaked thin Leonard. "She meets my purposes, but she's not a 'nice girl.' There are no 'nice girls' here. I'll ask again," the flat topped mastodon inched closer to Sam, "who are you really looking for?"

Big and Slim were too close for Sam to reach for his gun, draw it, and shoot more than one of them. It wouldn't do to simply pull the weapon and bark for more space, either. Sam knew he would lose a fight against a man as big as Dimitry in such a confined space. He needed to keep the conversation going.

"Okay, you got me," Sam laughed, holding both hands in the air. "I wasn't looking for a nice girl. I like my women like my martinis and I wanted to find the girl Charles met. Gayle. He said she's a regular. Brown hair cropped real short, turned up nose? She sounded like a real doll and I was hoping to swing in and get to know her. Maybe rob old Chuck of his prize. If I'd have known Charles had such loyal, protective and," he looked up to Dimitry, "big friends, I'd have just taken in a movie."

"Gayle," Leonard said without mirth. "She isn't here tonight. You wouldn't get to speak with her if she was."

Dimitry popped his knuckles. Things were getting hot. Sam pushed a foot against the table's metal support pole. The surface of the table rocked, though Leonard and Dimitry seemed not to notice. A wave of relief came to Sam. He could do something with a table that wasn't bolted to the floor.

"Look Leonard," Sam said, "forget I said anything. I'll just call it a night and head out. A round on me as I go. Whaddya say?"

"I sincerely doubt," Leonard said in a full nasal, "that you'll speak with Gayle any time soon, Mister Rockwell. Or is that supposed to be Detective Rockwell?"

Sam's face went blank.

"Don't act so surprised. We know all about what you want, and what your father lost."

The big man put a massive hand on the table and spoke in a heavy, Russian accent. "Why not you be telling us where to find?"

"Find what?" A rising panic coursed through Sam's innards. He heard a metallic clink. A gun? Switchblade? He didn't want to be stabbed or shot, so it really didn't matter all that much.

Using the table as leverage, he pulled it hard towards him, the table's round top bouncing against Dimitry's chest before it careened onto floor. The big Russian's air escaped with an "Ooof!"

At the same moment, Sam launched himself up from the booth and vaulted his knee into the thin man's face. The blow struck with a wet crunch and Sam knew Leonard's nose was broken. One done with, at least.

The force of Sam's strike made him fall with the thin man, who was sprawled out with legs drooping to the floor while his torso squirmed on the vinyl bench, pinned beneath Sam's weight. Sam could feel the thin man's teeth grinding beneath his knee. He heard another crunch, dryer this time.

He looked to his left and saw Dimitry inadvertently crush his partner's drinking glass. The big Russian shook away the shock and confusion of the attack and reached to grab hold of Sam. His swipe missed and Sam leapt from the booth and sought to exit the tavern.

A shouting morass of regulars formed a barricade, preventing Sam from reaching The Working Man's only door. Sam felt a flurry of hands grab and swing him around to face Dimitry. The Russian Bear writhed in anticipation. A circle of men formed, clamoring for a brawl.

From over his shoulder, Sam watched Leonard's girl wiping up torrents of blood from the thin man's shattered nose. The towering Dimitry lifted a rippling right arm and cocked his fist. He loosed a forceful punch aimed at Sam's head.

Sam nimbly ducked to his left and landed two sharp hooks to the big man's ribs. He heard a snap he hoped were the giant's ribs. A burning pain in his left hand told him otherwise. Dimitry attempted to respond with a backhand swat, looking to squish the fly he missed in his first salvo. Sam again easily ducked and cannoned a right cross toward Dimitry's exposed jaw. The Soviet's massive bear paw swatted the punch away and Sam settled for a quick jab to his opponent's bread basket. Fire bloomed in Sam's left hand at the point of contact. The punch hurt its target far less than it hurt Sam.

A massive boot slammed into Sam's chest, and the detective backpedaled from the force of the larger man's kick. A cheer went up from the crowd at their favorite's first strike. A sea of hands from the clamoring crowd halted Sam's backpedaling retreat. Dimitry issued a raw and throaty laugh.

Advancing, the big man let loose a wild haymaker with his left. Sam remained too swift and caught his opponent square on the back of the jaw with a savage uppercut. Dimitry's head swung violently from the blow.

The punch stunned both Dimitry and the crowd, whose slack mouths disclosed their surprise. Sam hammered his right fist again and again into the giant's face. Blood speckled Dimitry's mouth and trickled from his nose. The monster held up his hands in only the faintest imitation of a defensive guard. His eye began to swell as Sam struck with the thundering fury of a blacksmith on his anvil.

The end of the fight was near.

Sam reached back to deliver a knockout blow, only to feel his arm restrained. He turned to see Leonard, still holding a towel to his battered nose, pulling with all his might against Sam's cocked fist. Sam attempted to shrug the thin man off when another man wearing a black stocking cap attempted to grab his other arm. Sam rewarded the interloper with a sharp elbow, cutting him just above the eye.

Shouts of foul play erupted from some in the crowd and were met by cries of support for Dimitry and Leonard. The Working Man soon teemed with hard scrabble men pushing, jawing, and fighting among themselves.

Sam wrestled himself loose in the chaos and again sought to escape, only to be restrained again. He turned, ready to fight off another half-drunk truck driver. Instead he saw Dimitry holding him by the collar with a meaty hand. Sam's stomach sank. He attempted to wriggle out of his coat as two more grappled him.

The trio forced Sam to his knees, both arms held tightly behind his back. He continued to struggle for freedom as Leonard, the thin man, squinted at the blood-soaked bar towel he held. "Put 'im down for good, Dimitry," he said through his broken nose. "But make it look like it happened in da brawl."

Sam watched, helpless as Dimitry pulled back the frozen turkey he called a fist. The big Russian's mouth was open. An eye tooth was missing.

Did I do that?

Sam smiled in spite of the situation. He really could fight as good as the detectives in the books. Dimitry's punch landed like a fastball in a catcher's mitt, right where fat Salvatore Brunetti got him two nights ago. Sam saw darkness, then stars. He felt an explosion inside his head. Sirens rang loud in his ears. His chin hit hard against the splintery dirt on the beer-stained cedar floor.

And, just before the final blackness came, he thought, "Why couldn't he have aimed for the other side of my face?"

CHAPTER SEVEN

A room full of typewriters chattered and clicked incessantly. Sam instinctively examined his face. There was no pain, not even where Brunetti, then Dimitry, let him have it. He felt his chest and sides for broken ribs. His hands fumbled across his neck tie and he paused when he found it tucked between the buttons of his shirt.

Sam looked down. He was dressed in his old U.S. Army service uniform. He realized he was sitting down. A pair of wooden crutches leaned against his desk.

At first, Sam thought Dimitry had broken his neck and sent him to see the Pearly Gates Administration building first-hand. Further inspection proved otherwise. Six desks were split in two columns of three, facing the room's only door. A flag mounted on a heavy brass pole and stand filled the room's front corner.

Sam sat at the desk nearest to the secretary, a workspace he had occupied years before. He was in an administration building all right, but it wasn't anywhere near heaven. Sam was somehow back in Fort Bragg, North Carolina.

Possibilities and questions raced through his mind. Who flew him to North Carolina, or, a pretty solid impression of it? The last time he was here, he was convalescing from the wound he received as part of the 504th Infantry at Anzio.

If this was a re-creation who did it and why? Did it have something to do with his father's dossier of atomic secrets? Were Dimitry and Leonard waiting in custody at some holding cell? Had Gayle and Cox, who Sam was sure tipped his buddies off, been apprehended as well? How long had he been out of it?

But then, why would he be sitting in his old uniform at his old desk if he had here-to-fore been unconscious? He became aware that the room was empty. The clickety typing sounds ceased with the realization. Sam looked up in wonder at the newfound silence when the door opened. A sour-faced woman with pink lipstick and a protruding, masculine jaw took her seat at the secretarial desk. She left the door open.

"Captain Walters?" asked Sam.

The woman took no notice. She was stationed at Fort Bragg when Sam was last there, nearly nine years ago. She couldn't have been more than two years shy of retirement back then. What was going on, some sort of Soviet trick? Did Dimitry grab him and hand him over to the KGB? Was this an elaborate reconstruction designed to transform him into some sort of double agent? Or was that the detective novels and comic books talking?

An odd affection took Sam as he looked at Captain Walters. She wrote something in a ledger on her desk, licking the lead of her pencil every few sentences. The last time Sam had seen his brother Elijah, she had been in the room. Sam looked to the day calendar on the corner of his desk, it read May 19th, 1944. The sight startled him and Sam let loose a yelp. Walters didn't seem to notice.

Hanging above the door was a clock. It showed 12:22. The time was burned into Sam's memory—the exact moment his brother first appeared to him at Fort Bragg. As if on cue, a marine walked on stage, standing in the open door-frame wearing his sage green battle dress uniform.

Elijah!

Sam tried to spring from his seat to embrace his brother, but couldn't move. Captain Walters raised an eyebrow to Elijah. "A little far from Quantico, aren't you Marine?"

A sense of déjà vu rippled through Sam's brain. The scene before him was playing back like a movie reel. Sam knew what came next. His brother would joke with Captain Walters and then call him over.

"You don't know the half of it, lady," Elijah said, exactly as he had years before. "Sam, your nose is too close to that typewriter. Forget the paperwork and give your big brother a hug."

Sam remained bound to his seat like a public drunk put in the stocks. And then, he saw himself, still a soldier. The soldier Sam was years younger and wore a white cast over much of his leg. Sam realized he was a silent observer of his own past, like Ebenezer Scrooge at Fezziwig's ball.

Soldier Sam swung himself out of the seat and used the crutches to propel himself toward Elijah. "Elijah?" said the former Sam. "They found you? What are you doing here?"

The young Sam steadied himself on his crutches and reached out with his arm to pull his brother close for a hug. From his seat, Sam winced. He knew what was coming next. Young Sam passed through Elijah, barely stopping his fall by grabbing the sturdy brass flag pole. The pole wobbled as Elijah burst into fits of laughter. Captain Walters, believing Sam to have tripped, jumped from her desk to help.

"I'm sorry, Sammy," Elijah said through chuckles. "That was too good to resist."

Captain Walters and the younger Sam wore twin looks of confusion. Seeing the need for a better explanation, Elijah wiped away his smile. "No one found me," he said. "I'm pushing up daisies back on one of those damned Marshall Islands. I couldn't tell you which one. Caught a Jap bullet," he tapped a finger against his heart, "right here."

Captain Walters tottered over backwards and fell into a faint. Both brothers looked down to her on the floor, and then back at one another. Sam went to revive the Captain.

"Let her sleep," Elijah said. "She'll be all right. I wanted to talk with you in private, anyways." He glanced up hastily. "I don't know how much time I have."

Young Sam listened to his brother. He always listened to his brother. "You're dead?"

"Afraid so, but don't worry. I ran into a fella from my unit, Skip Hultz. He died the day after me. Said the Jap that got me was blown to hell a couple seconds later."

"Oh," said Sam, rubbing his arm.

"Yeah. I looked for the bastard up and down the hall but couldn't find him. Was going to give him a piece of my mind." Elijah let out a sigh. "I guess he was just doing his job, same as me. Maybe he went straight down. Or maybe they keep enemy combatants separated in the Pearly Gates Building. I ran into a Redcoat from the Revolutionary War. He said he didn't see any American colonists until he'd been in the hall for months."

"The Pearly Gates building," Sam said. "I can't believe you were there."

"Where'd you think they'd send me?" Elijah said, frowning at his little brother. "I may not have won as many Scripture memory awards, but I could hold my own. I wasn't getting sent down."

"Not that," Sam said, shaking his head. "I mean... I don't know what I mean. You're dead?"

"Dead as a doornail, little brother. But I don't mind. We all gotta go sometime, right? I'm eager to take the elevator upstairs to be honest."

"Oh, so... Why are you here?"

"To see you," Elijah said, throwing his arms out wide. "Believe me, I had to put my work in to get here. I died in February you know."

"Mom and Dad still think you're M.I.A."

"Afraid you'll have to set them straight."

Young Sam drooped his head, clearly not relishing the idea of bearing such bad news. "Why not visit Mom or Dad yourself? I bet they'll take the news a lot better straight from you."

"Can't. I only got the okay to see you. I told 'em that I had some crucial information to pass. It took a while but they eventually took my word for it. They're swamped with the war, you know."

"I bet."

"Everything is all out of sorts up there," Elijah continued. "Do you know they sent me to Anzio first? I scared a Colonel half to death before he told me that the 504th was pulled back to Naples."

Young Sam nodded. "Not me. I got sent stateside after Kraut arty busted up my leg. So what's the message?"

Elijah sat on top of an empty desk, the chinstraps from his helmet dangling wildly as he adjusted himself. "Let me finish my story," he said. "I didn't want to wander through Italy to find you. I thought about going AWOL and trying to haunt the Fuhrer, but they would have noticed and recalled me. So, I spooked a records clerk and got him to tell me that you were on a hospital ship headed stateside."

"Let me guess," Sam said, glancing again at Captain Walters. She was still out. Young Sam rested on a desk of his own. "You stowed away on some cargo barge and sailed after me."

"Good idea," nodded Elijah. "Actually I got recalled once the boys upstairs figured out I wasn't with you. I cooled my heels a few more weeks in the hall. Finally, a red-suited courier, like a bellhop at a fancy hotel, gives me a note and sends me straight to Fort Bragg. And here I am."

Young Sam looked at his brother straight-faced. "You should've haunted Hitler, maybe get him to jump out a window— from the top floor."

"I wouldn't have gotten away with it." Elijah said, standing up from the desk. "They'll haul you back up the moment they figure you're fooling 'em. You either do what they send you down to do, or you head back up and wait."

"Wait for how long?" Sam said. Captain Walters began to stir. Sam moved to attend to her. Elijah held up his palm, telling Sam to let her be.

"Just another minute," Elijah said. "To answer your question; real long. I saw a pioneer up there one day, wearing a coonskin cap and everything."

Still glued to his seat, the present Sam Rockwell smiled at his older brother. If he had a lot to say and little time to say it, you could count on Elijah to flap his lips incessantly. It used to drive their mother crazy. Present day Sam watched intently. "The pitch" was coming. Sam strained his ears to take in this pivotal moment in his past.

"So listen," said Elijah to young Sam. He leaned in, ready to convey a secret. Just like before the war separated the brothers. "I told you how busy it is up there. My case worker says that things are changing."

Young Sam gave his brother a quizzical look. Elijah nodded and said, "Folks have returned in the past, sure. We've all heard the stories. But with the war and what's coming down the road there's going to be a whole lot more of them and that's where you come in, little brother."

"Come in how?"

"Being a Return isn't a piece of cake. It's hard to get things done when you're immaterial. They know that upstairs and have made plans to get that taken care of. My caseworker said there'd soon be a lot of work for anyone alive that has a talent for helping the departed. Take it from me, little brother; become a private eye, like a Dick Tracy for ghosts. With all the Returns set to come, you'll be up to your ears in money."

"You returned to give me business advice?"

"Listen Sammy, I'm all set. But you? You've got a life to live. I want my little brother to live in style. Just get licensed and you won't know what to do with all the moolah coming your way. Pennies from heaven, only the real thing."

Young Sam rubbed his chin, but his older self was piqued by his brother's words.

Did Elijah say "licensed?"

Present day Sam didn't remember that part of the conversation. He wished desperately to be heard and ask a few questions. So far he hadn't seen any of the wealth or success Elijah had promised. But maybe the fault was his. He certainly didn't have a license. At least he'd met Amelia. He just needed to figure out how to keep her around until there was enough money for marriage.

"Look," said Elijah. Both past and present Sam snapped to attention. "I'm feeling the same funny feeling that came before they recalled me last time. I'm guessing my time is almost up. Tell Mother I love her and tell Dad that there's more to life than pot roast."

Elijah chuckled at his own joke.

"How am I supposed to figure out how to be a detective?" asked young Sam.

"I dunno, read up on how it's done. You're smart, Sammy. You'll do good."

Present day Sam watched as his brother disappeared. Until whatever today was, Sam had not seen Elijah, except in dreams.

Dreams! Maybe Amelia was onto something about his dreams being important when they involved Returns. He thought of his dream of the Italian Returns the night before, it was just as vivid as what he was experiencing now.

The thought vanished as Captain Walters propped herself up on both elbows. It was just the same as he remembered it. The Captain's next line should have been, "Did I faint?" Instead, she opened her mouth and repeated, "Rockwell. Rockwell. Rockwell."

The room faded into a blinding, buzzing white glow.

CHAPTER EIGHT

A rush of adrenaline split Sam's eyelids open. His vision was blurred, as if petroleum jelly covered his corneas. A man-shaped blob moved its mouth, but all Sam could hear was a steady, electric buzz.

Was that a dream? Was he still dreaming?

A bolt of lightning-like pain scorched the nerves in his cheek and echoed into his sinuses. Sam dropped his jaw open in silent protest of the hurting.

Not dreaming, he thought.

"Just... easy... Rockwell... okay?" said a voice. The words cut in and out as if controlled by a toddler spinning a radio's volume knob.

Full blast. Mute. Full blast. Mute.

Someone hoisted Sam to his feet. He tried to walk but his legs felt like they were buried under six feet of wet sand. He became aware that two men carried him under the arms. For a moment he thought it might be Dimitry and Leonard, but soon dismissed the thought. Whoever held him up, they were much less rough than those two would have been.

A sense of safety engulfed Sam. Sunlight after leaving a darkened theater, the horror movie over. He looked up to a blurry mirage of hot lights. The water in his eyes muddled something big and blue. Sam wiped with his sleeve and clarity came.

Moths plinked against hot bulbs illuminating a paint-peeled placard. He read a sign in a throaty croak. "The Working Man."

Straightening himself, Sam felt that he was standing under his own power. The hands of whoever had helped him along remained to steady him for a moment, then released.

Detective Clemons wheeled himself before Sam, appearing much too close.

Sam stepped backwards. He began to stumble. A hand thrust squarely between his shoulder blades, restoring his balance. Sam flashed an appreciative smile to the flatfoot behind him. This must be how most of the Working Man's patrons felt when leaving for home.

The place was thick with Cops. Officers pulled swollen-faced men from the bar in handcuffs. More police hastily scribbled eyewitness accounts of the night's earlier pandemonium. Sam saw more than one finger point in his direction. Swell.

"Barroom brawls," said Clemons, "a regular part of your detective work?"

"I only started it," Sam said, swabbing the inside of his mouth with his tongue, looking for blood and loose teeth.

"Hilarious," Clemons deadpanned. "The other fella finished it pretty well. You look awful, Rockwell."

"Me look awful? That's impossible, just ask my mother." His balance wavered slightly. Sam held out his arms to keep from falling over. "And let the record show that it was fellas, not fella. Plural, not singular. I had 'em licked so long as it was one at a time."

"Write that down Officer Dalton."

The officer standing behind Sam grunted an affirmative, but kept his pen in his pocket.

"So what brought you to this fine establishment?" Detective Clemons said, his arms folded and head tilted up expectantly. "Don't tell me you were thirsty."

Sam caressed his tender left cheek. Lieutenant Clemons knew this already. He'd better play along all the same. "Charles Cox told me about it," he said. "This is where he met the girl I think was in the office the night Frank was murdered."

"So what happened?" Clemons asked.

Sam found a bare patch of The Working Man's shingled wall to lean against. "Right when I walked in," he said, "a nervous string bean and his trained Russian bear took an interest. I tried to play coy about the girl—her name's Gayle, don't know a last name—and they decided to play it rough." He pushed himself from the wall and stared down at the Detective. "I'm on the right track with this Gayle dame, Lieutenant." He sounded like a giddy schoolgirl explaining his discovery.

Clemons pushed his hat to the back of his head, a flame of red hair erupting from underneath. He looked to Officer Dalton. "The fight must've softened Detective Rockwell's voice."

Sam kicked himself for forgetting to be in character. "Must've been hit in the throat," Sam said, reintroducing his charcoal growl.

Clemons frowned. "Where's your father, Sam?"

"I thought you took him home."

"No, I was called in and had to leave right away. Frank said he'd find a way home, gave me a sarcastic thanks for my public service."

"That sounds like him," Sam said. "Did he not make it home? Did you call my mother?"

"She hasn't seen him."

Sam felt the detective eyeball him like a stray dog that chanced upon an alley cat. This was his turf, his street, and from the way things sounded, he was tired of Sam's presence.

"Look, I'd love to help you Lieutenant, but you've seen him more recently than me."

"Did your father know anything about this place?" Clemons nodded to the washed out cedar shingles hanging loosely on The Working Man. "Did he give any sign of recognition when Cox mentioned the name?"

Frank Rockwell enjoyed a drink, Sam knew, but usually at home or with his friends. His father didn't generally associate with the sort of men who couldn't be bothered to clean their cuticles. Sam doubted Frank had ever been inside the leaning den of iniquity behind him. "No signs," he said.

"How about you?" Clemons said, moving into Sam's personal bubble. "You ever been here before?"

"No." Sam said, looking at Officer Dalton to try and get some read on the situation. The officer's face provided no clues.

"Tell me again how you knew exactly where to find those high heel prints in your father's office."

Sam sharpened up. Clemons wasn't just bothered by the commotion and this was not an aggravated exchange of information. The Lieutenant wasn't gruffly seeking Sam's help in the investigation, he was investigating Sam.

"A hunch," Sam said, keeping his voice hard and crossing his arms. "You think I killed my father?"

"No," Clemons said. He squinted, and freckled crow's feet enfolded his eyes. "What does Gayle look like?"

Sam searched his memory for the description he wrote earlier, then stopped. The detective was right next to him when that brunette employee of his father stated the facts. Clemons hadn't forgotten. Was this an accusation? "You think I'm in cahoots with the girl?" he asked.

"I think," Clemons said calmly, "you should try and answer my question."

A drunken machinist evacuated cheap rum over the side of the pier in gasping fits. The wind shifted, giving Sam a whiff that added to the turmoil he already felt inside. He'd somehow gone from a trustworthy detective to a murder suspect. And right at the center of a barroom brawl to boot. This was getting better and better.

"Look, Lieutenant," Sam said, his voice channeling the pulp detectives, "you want to bring me in then bring me in, but let's cut out the dancing."

"Or what?" snarled Clemons. He pulled back his jacket and placed his hands on his hips, pushing his chest in Sam's direction.

Clemons was taller than average, but still a few inches shorter than Sam. "Cut the Dick Tracy act," he said. "It might work on a bunch of lily-livered souses, but not me."

Sam blanched. "How'd you know?" he blurted, the words escaping his lips before his brain had a chance to evaluate whether they were best left unsaid.

"You act like you're acting. And you sound like you smoked sixty years' worth of cigarettes and then swallowed a bowl of nails."

"It's not that bad—"

"It's an act and I see right through it." Clemons began pacing. "You do what I do long enough and you can pick out phonies the way your granny picks fruit at the market. Come clean, son. What's your connection with Gayle?"

The flint-like voice Sam queued up disappeared in his throat. "No connection, Lieutenant," he said in his natural pattern of speech. "Just trying to find out who murdered my father."

Detective Clemons pushed his hat to the farthest ends of his head, his red hair obscuring most of it. He drew a pale, freckled hand across his face and pulled down, as if trying to take off his own cheeks. "Follow me upstairs, Rockwell."

A flash sent whirling spots spinning before Sam's eyes as a photographer captured images of the crime scene. A single lamp provided the room's only other light, overpowered with every POOMP! POOMP! of the photographer's flashbulb.

The room smelled of stale spirits and something else.

Something sweet and foul at the same time. Sam rubbed his eyes to take in the scene. A small fogged window was propped open by a wooden spoon. The floor was thick with grime and Sam's shoes made a SKITCH sound with each step. The floor sought to claim his oxfords for its own.

A decrepit bed, sagging in the middle from a broken frame boasted every stain imaginable. A man with a white coat, like a scientist just let loose from the lab, pulled the covers of the bed back with a pair of tongs.

In the corner was a chair with a white sheet resting over it. It took Sam a moment to realize a body sat in eternal repose underneath. Lieutenant Clemons took hold of the sheet and waited for Sam to join his side. With his eyes fixed on Sam, the detective pulled back the cover and revealed a pale face of death. It was a young woman, a trickle of blood ran from her nose and the corner of her mouth.

Sam studied the woman's face and then looked to the Lieutenant, eager to see what Clemons had to say.

"You know this girl?" asked Clemons.

"No," said Sam. He used his own voice, and wondered at how small it sounded.

Clemons studied Sam intently for several long moments. Finally, he sighed and pulled the sheet back over the corpse. "I believe you," he said. "Sorry to have to expose you to this. Not something you run into regularly in your line of 'detective work' is it?"

Sam shook his head. "Returns are always cleaned up. But it's not the first time I've seen a dead body. How did she die?"

"Nothing obvious. Morgue'll have to figure it out. You can

probably smell the booze in her." Detective Clemons presented Sam with a thick envelope, aged yellow. "We found this in her purse."

The envelope was full of hand-written notes on stationary. Sam pulled out a random page. He recognized his father's handwriting. "My dearest Ally," the note began; a love letter to Sam's mother. He flipped the devotional over and found Alice's gushing reply. This must have been one of the items taken from his father's office safe. Funny that his old man would keep it there. He never seemed like the type.

Sam stuffed the letter back in its envelope and considered the body under the white sheet. "My father's murderer," he said.

The fresh air outside of The Working Man revived Sam physically. Detective Clemons had called him out, but already Sam's confidence was returning. The vibrant noise of the city and police as they cleared the area energized him. He rolled his neck, and heard his vertebrae pop and crack. He would solve this case.

After all, it was he who found Gayle's heel prints and followed the clues to the dive behind him. He found some kind of connection between his father's secret dossier and the pair of thugs. It probably wasn't a coincidence that the big one spoke with a Russian accent. Frank's killer was dead. Sam took deep breaths of the salty air. He had done it. Not his character. Him.

He could unravel the rest of the case, too. Clemons could use him, Sam was sure of it. He'd drop the act and still get the job done. "Listen to this," said Sam, "Why don't we put out an alert for the two bozos that tangled with me and see if they know anything about what happened to the murderer. I know for certain that I broke the skinny one's nose. I might have cracked a couple of the big man's ribs. It was probably just my hand, though." He tried to flex his slightly swollen fingers. They hurt. "Maybe they'll stop by Saint Joe's to get patched up."

"Sorry, you're out," Clemons gave back. "You're not working this case. You're an amateur and a liability. Just be glad we've found someone who can credibly back up your version of the fight."

"What?"

"Everyone we've talked to says you started the fight. But that's where the similarities end. Most of them say no one fitting the descriptions of your two goons were there. A couple of them say you walked in the front door and took a swing at the barkeep."

"That's ridiculous."

"I'm not done. Most of them say the fight broke out in the back of the room, but everyone joined in before long."

"So what, I'm in trouble again?" Sam shifted his weight from one foot to the next.

"Not yet," said Clemons. "Like I said, I believe you didn't know Gayle and that you weren't in on your father's murder. Enough drunks slurred out confirmations of a big guy getting walloped by a 'smaller big guy.' Maybe that's you."

"It is."

"The fact that we found your father's suspected killer dead upstairs keeps me from having you hauled off with the rest of these drunks."

"So what now?"

"Go home. But stick around in case I need to talk to you. I'll let the fighting slide. Consider it payback for tracking this place down."

"You said to do what needed to be done."

"I didn't think you'd do it like this. I can deal with one drunk getting squeezed. Not a bar full of them." Clemons turned and made for his car.

Sam sighed and followed the detective. "Any chance you can drive me to Cox's place, Lieutenant? I need to pick up the Cadillac."

"Yeah, sure."

"And it wouldn't be a bad idea to see if he has anything to say about my fight with Abbott and Costello."

"All right, maybe I'm being a bit rash. You can have a look with me by your side, but don't push it."

A wave of nausea boiled over Sam. He pressed his palm against his forehead.

"You sure you're up to a drive?"

The sickness passed and Sam shook loose more cobwebs. "Beats walking."

Sam rubbed his throbbing knuckles while Clemons poked through a stack of overturned magazines. Cox's apartment was empty.

He had followed Clemons into the building, taking his silence as assent. Sam was fairly certain the detective would have told him to scram if he really didn't want him around. Maybe his work earned him some grace. Results are results, his father would say.

The building superintendent waited outside as Sam and Clemons examined emptied out drawers and overturned furniture. Clemons stooped to take a look at the coffee table, still tipped on its side from Cox's frightened kick at Frank's sudden appearance. "This looks like the only real sign of a struggle," he said.

"It's not, though. He knocked it over in fright when my father appeared in the room. Cox didn't know he Returned when he left the office."

"Okay," Clemons said, picking up a loose sheet of paper and tossing it aside when it provided no value. "And let the record show that it's only because you can tell me those sorts of details that I let you come with me. You're still off this case."

Sam nodded. For now, he thought.

"Well, if it wasn't someone else who sent this over end," Clemons gestured to the table, "then Cox was in a hurry to get out of here. Didn't even bother to set the table upright again before he left. I can't stand untidy people."

"It's a real epidemic with youth today."

"Don't get funny. You've made my life untidy, Rockwell. Your little pet detective agency provided a lead, sure, but this," he waved at walls, "this is sloppy work that I'm going to have to follow up. Cox was probably right on your heels out the door. A real detective would have stuck around to see if he tried to fly the coop, especially if he gave as much cause for suspicion as you said."

"Sorry, Lieutenant."

"A lot of good that does me. I could've put someone across the street to keep watch if you had brains enough to know what you were looking for."

Sam winced. He hadn't trusted Cox. Maybe the time spent waiting and watching for him wouldn't have made a difference in what happened at the tavern. Sam thought he played a good detective, but didn't seem able to act his way into making sound investigative choices. He either hit, or in this case, missed big. But at the same time, Clemons knew right well what Sam was up to.

"I figured the action would be at the tavern," Sam said, his hands still apologizing. He kicked at a potted plant. "And it was. Still, I knew Cox was hiding something. So Cox, Gayle, and the other two are together. When I came inside The Working Man, the first thing the pencil neck asked was if I was sympathetic. Come to think of it, that's how they beat around asking if you're a communist in Hollywood, too."

"The Working Man," Clemons said, shaking his head. "Nothing like subtlety. You're making sense in spite of yourself."

"Gee, thanks," Sam said, keys to the Cadillac already in his hands.

The two men exited the apartment and left the superintendent to lock up. The super jiggled the door handle, verifying that it locked properly. "You think he skipped out on me?" he said.

"I wouldn't hold my breath waiting for next month's rent," Sam said as he trailed Detective Clemons. The two men took the stairs, leaving the Super in the hall. The night air greeted Sam as the Lieutenant opened the door and Sam made straight for his father's Cadillac.

"Sam," Clemons called. Sam paused at the car door. "It looks like you put us on the right trail. I want to ask you a couple of questions, but don't get the idea that you're a part of this case any longer. I'm almost ready to forgive you for misleading me, but I'm not making you a partner in this."

"Glad to help, Detective."

"The FBI called back after we wired them a list of your father's clients. No one on that list would have had any access to the sort of classified information he's been talking about."

Sam's eyebrows went up. "You think he's faking about the atomic secrets? Why would he do that?"

"How should I know? Is it possible that he has another list of clients, maybe something confidential?"

"I couldn't say. Sorry."

Clemons chewed his lip. "If this is a case of espionage, what are the odds your father worked with the Russians to get that dossier?"

Sam felt a snicker claw its way up his abdomen, breaking free with a deep bellied laugh that echoed down the empty street. The outburst combined with his infectious smile brought a wave of pain and cut the funny out of him. He held his stomach with his right hand and his bruised face with his left. With a long, contented sigh he said, "My father is the last man that would do anything remotely dangerous. Besides, he hates communists like Adlai Stevenson hates television."

"You laugh," said Clemons, "but I've got to look at all the angles. Maybe he takes a payoff and gets double crossed. He cons them upstairs and they send him back to rewrite the story, leaving out anything that might tarnish his legacy."

Sam opened his father's Cadillac and said, "Something happened involving my father, Cox, and a girl that enjoyed the company of communists. But I guarantee my father wasn't on the wrong side of things. I'm going to drive home and see if he's there."

"Given your track record when it comes to telling me the truth, detective, your guarantee doesn't mean much to me." Clemons left Sam and entered his blue Packard.

Sam keyed the ignition and reached over to roll down the passenger window. He idled the car forward until he was parallel with Clemons' car. "He's not a spy, Lieutenant."

"Every minute the FBI doesn't flood this town makes me think your father isn't on the up and up. We'll see, Sam."

CHAPTER NINE

Frank stood idly on the street for several moments after Detective Clemons drove off in response to a call. "Abandoning me with no way to get home," he said to himself. He had, of course, demurred to the dispatcher's request, but he was just being polite. The decent thing would have been for Clemons to race Frank home and then take care of whatever new police matter had popped up.

It seemed no one had any respect for the dead.

In no mood to walk back home all the way from downtown, Frank remembered how Eamon sent him straight home from his office in the Pearly Gates Admin Building. Frank looked up to the sky. "How about a lift back home?"

No reply. He wasn't surprised. Frank had grown accustom to unanswered prayers, which is why he seldom offered any. Besides, he was fairly certain he once heard a sermon about the error of praying to any but God alone. Probably during that last Easter service Alice forced him to attend.

Frank clucked his tongue. Pastor Barnaby never preached a sermon that had to do with the Holiday at hand. All the more reason to boycott the pews. But, if Barnaby was right that prayers were for God only, asking Eamon for help might get him in trouble. He was already dead and didn't want to press his luck. He thought about praying to the Almighty directly, but it didn't seem fit to ask to be lifted up and set back down in his own living room. Frank began to walk down the hill toward Pacific Avenue.

He reached the busy street just as evening gave way to night, though the horizon still held enough purple-pink light to render the street lamps unnecessary. Frank would just float if he tripped, anyway. The city street buzzed with cars while the sidewalks were packed with people eager for dinner or the theater. Frank stood just in front of a newly converted hotel.

A group of nuns exited a bus and Frank thought briefly about taking their place. He had no way of paying the required dime and scrapped the plan. A taxi lolled down the street looking for a customer. "No upfront money needed," thought Frank. He raised his hand to flag the cab down and nodded as the cabby pulled over.

Deciding it would be best not to let the driver know he was a spirit, he leaned into the open passenger window. "Mind helping me with my luggage?" Frank said. The driver might get spooked and leave him standing curbside if he knew Frank was a ghost.

The driver looked like a farmer who had lost his farm. He ambled out of the car in loose overalls and went to the rear of the vehicle. Obscured by the open trunk, Frank ghosted through the backseat and sat down next to a company jacket the cab driver was probably required to wear. Frank leaned out the door and called out, "I'm sorry, I forgot that my luggage was already taken up by an associate."

The old plowman shrugged. He closed the trunk with a hollow metallic thud and rambled back into his seat. Frank spent the ride in thankful silence. He instructed the driver to stop nearly a mile short of his home. That wouldn't be too long of a walk.

Pointing to the cab's meter, the driver held out an open palm expectantly.

"Sorry," Frank said as he passed out of the car. "I don't have any money. You can bill Rockwell Fiduciary for the fee, just mention Frank Rockwell."

The driver blinked a moment and exited the vehicle. "So you're one of them, huh?" he called out after Frank, who already began to walk home. Frank wasn't sure if "them" he meant dead or deadbeat. He hated being either, but walked on without comment.

Reaching out with a massive paw, the driver attempted to grab Frank's shoulder. It passed well into Frank's back. The cabby pulled his hand in as if snakebit and tucked it under his arm. The jilted cab driver let loose a slew of homespun profanity involving mules and coyotes then screeched off into the night.

Frank kept walking, eager to speak with Alice. His home was cheerfully lit when he arrived. An American flag lazily flapped in the night's summer breeze. Pastor Barnaby's relic of a car sat in the driveway. Frank wanted to avoid an encounter with the Parson and elected to walk around the block, hoping Barnaby would soon depart.

After a half dozen trips he began to feel like Joshua circling the walls of Jericho. Didn't that Pastor have an appointment with a prayer closet somewhere? Frank continued his circuits around the block. As he walked, he thought about Samuel.

It might not be entirely safe for his untested detective of a son to go looking for murderers in a seedy waterfront tavern. Frank wondered if he should have accompanied his son, but determined he was correct not to. There wasn't much that he could do about any trouble, was there? At best he might give a gunman the goosebumps. No, Sam was more than capable of defending himself. He had always been a first rate fighter in and out of the boxing ring.

Turning a corner and arriving on his street once again, Frank's thoughts turned to Alice. How many more times would he be able to see her? If Sam solved his murder, or if Eamon started looking into things, it wouldn't be long. He needed to talk to his wife, let her know exactly how he felt.

But why couldn't she, why couldn't everybody, act like his death mattered? He'd worked slavishly his entire life in order to set his family up. He made sure no one would need a thing in life, or when he was gone. Couldn't Alice see how he had devoted his life to her? She never lacked for anything. Frank did his duty. He gave her cards when the occasion called for them, flowers as well. He was a good provider.

Looking up from his laces, Frank saw his home grow near. Barnaby's car was still in the driveway, but the time to come home was now. Frank stepped onto his lawn, the grass blue-emerald in the moonlight. The night sky told him that he'd walked for a long time. Hours?

Usually, Frank would develop blisters after thirty minutes of activity. Time went by quickly when fatigue no longer presented its visage. Welcome to eternity.

Front doors being no obstacle, Frank walked through his own and found Alice in the living room, laughing with Amelia and Pastor Barnaby. Time to get this over with. Frank gave a swift nod to the man whose sermons he avoided so earnestly in life and turned his attention to his wife.

"Frank, you're back," said Alice. "But where's Sam?"

"He wanted to follow a lead," Frank said. Then, forgetting himself, "Did you tell him he could drive my baby?"

Alice ducked her head and the trio laughed. Frank rooted himself in place, arms akimbo. "What's so funny?" he said.

"I'm sorry," said Pastor Barnaby, "your wife anticipated your response verbatim."

"What?" asked Frank.

"You reacted about the car exactly like she said you would," Amelia said, trying to be helpful.

"Don't be so grouchy, Frank," said Alice. "Amelia was telling us a story about how our son's theory on detective work nearly got him thrown off a pier by a pair of gangsters. We were already in a laughing mood."

Amelia blushed. "I only shared the story because Sam was able to fight them off. They weren't real gangsters in the end. Just a pair of grifters bothering a Return's nephew. Sam does all right, Mr. Rockwell."

"I should say so," said Frank. He strutted with pride over his son, completely forgetting the message he meant to deliver to his wife. "Samuel alone found the clue that put the police on the trail of…" Frank trailed off and bowed his head solemnly. "…my killer," he concluded, the final two words spoken so somberly that he was sure the company would join him in lamentations.

"That's wonderful," exclaimed Amelia. She and Alice beamed at the report while Pastor Barnaby nodded his white head in approval.

"Yes," said Frank. "I mean, no. Alice, why is everyone so… festive? Doesn't anyone feel bad that my beating heart has been stilled?" He began to pace back and forth, waving his hands.

"I grieve for the loss of all life," said Barnaby. "Please don't mistake my levity to mean that I approve of the detachment now popular among the living."

Alice shrugged off the Reverend's words. "Oh Frank, don't be so dramatic. I'll live what, another forty years at most? And then I'll see you again. It's really not something to be bothered about."

Frank puckered up his face and balled his fists, waving one in the air. "And what about giving Samuel the keys to my Cadillac? How could you?" He pointed a trembling finger at the Reverend. "Barnaby is a do-gooder, have him drive Samuel around town."

Amelia grew quiet, made uncomfortable by the brewing argument.

"Pastor had a prior appointment to keep," Alice said, rising to her feet. "I don't know why you're so bothered. Will Sam driving it hurt the resale value?"

"The resale value?" parroted Frank. He began to pace like an expectant father in the delivery ward. "When have I ever insinuated that I would sell my Cadillac, except to trade it in for a newer model?"

"Never," said Alice. She looked back at Amelia and Barnaby and sweetened her tone, hoping to keep her husband from exploding. "But I don't like driving a car that large. I thought I might sell it and buy one of those little Metropolitans with the pink top."

"Sell my car?!" yelled Frank, red-faced. It wasn't a question. "I'm murdered, murdered, for Pete's sake, and no one gives two damns and a glass of lemonade about it!"

Pastor Barnaby rose, looking sternly at Frank, who withered slightly under the glare. With a soft civility he said, "Frank, you've been murdered. That's a terrible affront to the living God. A violation of the sixth commandment. There may well be damnation for this sinful act, though I pray there is yet time for the culprit. Nevertheless, damnation is nothing to desire and you'd do well to consider the psalmist, 'keep thy tongue from evil.'"

"That does it," Frank hollered. He jumped in place and waved his fist through the air. "I've gone out of my way to avoid your sermonizing, Barnaby, and I won't listen to you preach in my home."

Amelia rose to exit the room, but Alice took her arm. "Frank," she said, "apologize to Amelia and Reverend Barnaby."

"I will not," he said, puffing out his chest, eyes closed. He opened one lid and aimed it at Amelia. "Sorry, Amelia."

Amelia pulled her hair behind her ear and gave a wave of acknowledgment, then looked down as she twisted the toe of her shoe on the carpet.

Tugging on his white haired temples, Barnaby smiled feebly at Alice. "I should apologize as well."

Franked nodded vigorously. "I admit," Barnaby said, "to knowing very little of the trials Returns such as you face, Frank."

Now calmed and idly examining his finger nails, Frank looked at the Reverend from beneath half-closed eyelids. "It's all righ—"

"I look to Scriptures," Barnaby interrupted, clasping his hands behind his back and stepping away from his chair. "There I find Lazarus, Samuel's ghost, those in Jerusalem at Christ's death, and our Savior's resurrections." He stopped in front of Frank, examining him. "Your case is nothing like those," he said. "Particularly the latter most."

Frank chortled and heard a snicker from Alice. He opened his mouth to retort, but Barnaby began anew. "However," he said, circling the room, "We can consider the case of Enoch to see that the Lord is sovereign and sovereignly He may change the pattern of our expectations. Perhaps that is the reason for your coming back. I won't say."

Frank let out a sigh. "That's all very interest—"

"But I will say this," Barnaby said, picking up the thought. "Whatever the Scriptures leave unsaid about what happens in between death and the final judgment, what is clear is this..." He paused as if for dramatic effect, in full pulpit delivery. All eyes were fixed on the Reverend.

"Well," Frank moaned, "spit it out."

"Man and wife become one flesh through marriage and remain so until death do them part. Your death has come, and Alice must be allowed to continue her life as best glorifies God. In regards to your Cadillac, I daresay that Alice being pressured to acquiesce to your worldly and material demands is not in that vein."

The room went silent as Frank stood rigid, his mouth gaping open. Silently, he held out a hand toward Reverend Barnaby, as if to say, Will you listen to this? Alice shifted her feet and wrung her hands. Amelia cleared her throat and again tried to leave the room.

"Nobody move," bellowed Frank. "I want witnesses for the sake of posterity. I have a new least favorite sermon of yours, Barnaby." He turned to his wife. "How many times, Alice, have I said that your Pastor was bent on telling me what to do? Well here's irrefutable proof. The nerve of telling me I can't tell my wife what to do with my own property."

Alice looked to the floor. "Frank," she said, "You're dead. I can't be expected to meekly let my life be run by a ghost. It's not fair to me."

A heavy silence filled the room.

"So, you all side with him, do you?" Frank shouted, a thick vein protruding from his forehead. "More money for the offering plate with me out of the way! Ho ho!"

Barnaby drew up, indignant. He opened his mouth to denounce the accusation but Frank spoke first. "Alice," he said "There's a knife in my back to replace the bullet that killed me. What's so blasted difficult about keeping a man's things exactly as he'd wish them to be after he dies?"

Amelia again tried to escape. "Excuse—"

"I was a good provider, Alice." Frank was rampaging next to the television cabinet, arms flailing. "You ought to wear black and mourn me for the rest of your days, like those little Mediterranean women downtown. Go to church and light a few candles for my soul."

The Reverend interjected. "Prayers for the dead are not in keeping with—"

"Clam it, Barnaby," said Frank. "I'm sorry I'm not worth mourning over, Alice. I'm a good provider. Amelia," Amelia looked at the floor awkwardly, unenthusiastic about being brought into the conversation. Frank didn't notice. "You're lucky Sam is so much like me. He'll make his way and give you everything you'll ever want. Sam knows how important it is to be a good provider!"

Alice stood in front of Amelia, as if shielding her from Frank. "You leave her and Samuel out of this, Frank Rockwell."

Frank waved a dismissive arm at his wife. "Why not tell the girl the truth?" he said. "Did I ever miss a birthday, or fail to sign a card, or forget to have flowers delivered? You act like I never did my duty." He poked a finger at his chest and moved toward Alice. "I did my duty."

"Maybe," Alice said, "I'd mourn over your loss if you provided me with a feeling of being more than a well-kept obligation. Maybe those tears you want so badly would come if you lived your life like I and our children were more than a duty to fulfill." She could feel tears threatening to come as she fumed, but held them back defiantly.

Frank stood acutely aware of another Barnaby glare. Alice looked as angry as he'd ever seen her and Amelia was fixated on the color of their rug. He was dumbfounded. How could his wife of so many years think she was something less than the very center of his world?

"What are you saying, Alice? Don't cry. I'm a good provider Alice! I'm a—"

Alice didn't hear the end of Frank's sentence; he disappeared with a suddenness that made Amelia and Reverend Barnaby jump. Both her guests joined her in the realization that her husband was definitely and completely called to the hereafter. She could feel the awkward tension that milled about in the room.

"Goodbye, Frank," she sighed.

Sam rose with the sun. He swung his legs out of bed and sniffed, hopefully not so loud to wake Amelia or his mother. He enjoyed the way his mother and Amelia fussed over his battle wounds when he came home last night. Especially Amelia.

Amelia and his mother told him his father was gone for good this time. He had just missed Reverend Barnaby. Sam told them about finding Gayle and guessed that Frank's disappearance coincided with her death. It still seemed to Sam as he stretched his tired muscles back to life, that the girls had held something back about his father.

Frank's funeral was scheduled for Saturday. It seemed soon. It hadn't been a day since Sam last talked with his father. The murder was on Wednesday, and the burial would be three days later.

The details of the case played out in Sam's mind like a Hitchcock dream sequence, only happy. Taking in the morning air from his open window, he quietly made his bed with military exactness. Finished, he put his hand on the wall separating his room from Amelia's. He needed to solve this case and make a name for himself. He needed to succeed and make a life with

Amelia.

He went to bed the night before as an optimist. And why not? Sam out-worked a properly trained detective, tracked down his father's killer, and fended off a pair of criminals that seemed to have crawled right out of the yellowed pages of one of his crime novels.

Lieutenant Clemons had been adamant about Sam being off the case. Yet, there was still a part of Sam that believed persistence might change the detective's mind. Surely Clemons would recognize what Sam accomplished.

Walking to the bathroom, Sam flexed his left hand. It was still tender, but not so bad that he'd require a doctor's visit. In the mirror he examined the butterfly bandages Amelia had placed over the cuts on his face. She said they made him look rugged and dashing. Sam shrugged his shoulders. He thought he looked like a tenderized steak, but if Amelia wanted to compliment his looks, he wasn't going to complain.

Entering the kitchen, there was an energy beneath Sam's feet, exploding up through his knees like fireworks on Independence Day. Sam wanted to run until his legs could move no longer, but felt so vibrant that doubted he would ever grow tired again. He heard Amelia or his mother stir upstairs and started to cook breakfast, sending eggs and bacon into a sizzling frenzy as their scents permeated the morning air.

Sam attended to the eggs and took a sip from his second cup of coffee when Amelia came downstairs, followed almost immediately by his mother.

"Something smells good," Amelia said. "I didn't know you could cook, Sam."

"I just go to those diners for the atmosphere."

"Good morning, Samuel," said Alice, politely assuming control of the kitchen. She served the food and joined Sam and Amelia at the breakfast table.

"Amelia, I was thinking." Sam pushed his empty plate toward the center of the table. "Would you like to see the mountain with me today?"

"Oh, I'd love that."

"It looks close, but it's a long drive," said Sam. "So we'd better start to get ready. I'll start packing a picnic."

"I'll help you, Samuel," said Alice. She called after Amelia, who was already moving for the stairs. "Be sure to take a sweater Amelia. It's summer but if the sun goes behind the clouds, you feel the chill from the elevation. There's almost always snow somewhere nearby.

"Thank you, Mrs. Rockwell." Amelia disappeared up the stairs.

"Well, I think this is a wonderful idea," said Alice as she fetched a wicker picnic basket from deep within a cupboard.

Sam opened the icebox and examined the contents, searching out what was most ripe for the plunder. "Yeah, it should be nice. Isn't Amelia wonderful?" He tossed a wedge of cheese into the open basket.

"You have to put the plates in first," Alice said, removing the cheese. "Why don't you just gather what you want to bring and let me do the packing?"

Sam went searching and came back with an armful of food. He unloaded his cargo on the table next to his mother.

"Samuel," said Alice, putting a jar of raspberry preserves in the wicker picnic basket, "I'm torn between two emotions right now. I'm proud of what you accomplished last night, tracking down your father's murderer."

"That's one," Sam said.

Alice gently stroked his battered face. "I'm also worried about your being a detective. I never imagined helping Returns would lead you into such dangerous situations. Have you ever thought about a career change? Maybe taking up the family business?"

"You mean work for Mrs. Alice Rockwell, new President of Rockwell Fiduciary?" Sam said with a chuckle. He tossed two small apples in after the preserves. They made the plates clatter against the silverware.

"You'll bruise them, Samuel. I went over your Father's will. Nothing's changed. He still wants you to take ownership of the company. It only goes to me if you refuse. But Samuel, I want the same."

Sam was surprised. His father had never mentioned anything like this to him, but the time they spent during his Return had been rather singularly focused. He felt unprepared for the task being urged on him. The only knowledge he had of the world of wealth is what he'd gleaned from his father. Lectures received while growing up and occasional conversations while in college. It was amazing how you could grow up with a man for most of your life and know nothing about what he did all day. Still, Sam didn't know the first thing about detective work either, and that hadn't stopped him.

"Think of it like this," Alice said, lowering her voice as she glanced to see if Amelia had yet returned downstairs, "you'll find yourself able to provide for a family much sooner this way."

Sam blushed. "I'll think it over after I find what those two communists are up to."

Alice ignored the comment. "Amelia is delightful, Samuel. You can't keep her waiting like this."

"I'm pretty sure she knows how I feel about her. I just need to become a good provider first, like father always said."

Alice winced as her son unknowingly echoed his father's final words. She put down the napkins she had been folding. "No woman wants to feel like a checklist needs finishing before she can be loved, Samuel."

"I'm not sure I..." Sam trailed off as Amelia lightly made her way down the stairs. Dressed in a white cotton dress with blue trim, she looked as if she were floating down the banister. Sam felt the sudden urge to inhale, and sputtered when he found his lungs could hold no more.

"I'm all ready," Amelia said, resplendent. Her words seem to draw all of the air from the room, and Sam felt warm and light. She was so very beautiful.

"You look lovely, Amelia," said Alice.

"Thank you, Mrs. Rockwell. Will you be joining us today?"

"I'm afraid not. Reverend Barnaby is taking me to see about finalizing the arrangements for Frank's funeral tomorrow. It's been short notice, but Frank's bank accounts combined with a Pastor's contacts are making things work out."

"We'd better get going if we want to reach Paradise by lunchtime," said Sam. "The earthly one, just below the mountain, not the heavenly place," he added to Amelia.

"Would you mind leaving the 'For Sale' sign in the Cadillac's window when you park?" asked Alice. "You never know when a potential buyer might be near."

Sam nodded an affirmative, took the picnic basket from his mother, and offered Amelia the crook of his elbow. She weaved her slender arm inside. "I was sure," Sam said, just loudly enough for his mother to hear, "that Father planned on being buried in that car."

Days' worth of conversation was crammed into the two-hour drive along the state highway. Sam provided a detailed account of the case so far, paying special attention to the fighting prowess he exhibited at The Working Man.

"I'm glad you weren't kidding about being able to fight." Amelia shook her head.

Grinning, Sam let his eyes leave the road momentarily to take in Amelia's profile. "I'm just thankful there weren't any overweight Italians around to knock me down."

Amelia laughed. "Let's thank heaven," she said. "But I still think the big one is more dangerous than Mr. Brunetti. Does it make you worry that he's out there somewhere?"

"Not particularly. I think the skinny one, Leonard, is the dangerous one."

They sat quietly, the adulations over a successful night ebbing away, revealing an unspoken but gnawing concern that these two men were loose. Sam didn't mention Gayle.

"Tell me what you think about my home state."

Amelia put a hand to her cheek. "It's lovely. One of the most beautiful places I've ever been."

"I'm not sure what possessed me to leave it." Sam stole another glance at Amelia. She met his eyes and he cooed, "But I'm glad I did."

Amelia pushed her hair behind her ears. "That's very sweet of you to say. I'm thankful, too."

The two grew quiet, taking in the wild and majestic world outside as the Cadillac glided along Paradise Valley Road. Amelia gasped at the lavender colored meadows teeming with wildflowers. Mount Rainier's icy peaks loomed above them and pockets of stalwart snow dotted the countryside, refusing to melt even before the intensity of the summer sun.

"It's lovely!" Amelia exclaimed. "I promise I'll never call anything in California a mountain again." Her hands were pressed against the dash and she leaned forward, craning her neck upward in a fruitless attempt to see the top of the regal volcano, beautiful in its slumber.

"Some may be taller," Sam pulled the car to the side of the road, "but none so beautiful as this one." He opened the door and helped Amelia out of the car, steadying her as she found her footing on the sloping gravel which cut a path between alpine fields.

Leading her down a faint footpath, Sam walked close to Amelia, the path just wide enough for the pair to travel side-by-side. Amelia threatened to take off in a frolicking gait, her body moving at a pace somewhere just under a skip. Sam's heart matched her every step with a skip of its own. He found a sun-drenched patch of green nestled among a waving sea of royal blue Penstemon wildflowers.

Amelia stretched out a brown and red blanket while Sam

opened the hinged lid of the picnic basket. His eyes bulged and a jolt of adrenaline crashed down his chest, ricocheting throughout his stomach. Sitting on the top of the bread and apples was a small, black velvet box. Sam knew at once that his mother had placed it there. He also knew what sparkled within. He pocketed the ring box while Amelia smoothed out the blanket.

Sam shook his head in disbelief, wondering what he would have said if Amelia was the one to open the basket. Perhaps that's what his mother was hoping for. Usually she only offered laments about having to wait for grandchildren. When it came to Amelia, she seemed to be taking a much more direct approach.

Looking up, Sam saw Amelia looking at him. He'd been standing dumbfounded by his mother's audacity. He gave a half-smile of acknowledgment, and quickly went to work removing the picnic from its basket.

"What do you think?" Sam said as he finished arranging the food.

"It looks delicious," said Amelia, reclining on her knees opposite Sam.

"No, I mean the mountain."

"I already told you that it's lovely."

"I know. I just wanted to hear you say that word again. Lovely."

"It is..." Amelia teased out the last word, "lovely."

They laughed, together. Sam buttered slices of bread, readying them for the preserves. He offered her the picnic's first-fruits, kneeling with all the solemnity of Governor Bradford at the first Thanksgiving. "Behold this bounty."

"Thank you," Amelia giggled.

An urge came over Sam to see if Amelia would come with

him on a different path. He went from his knees to sitting cross-legged, his pocket knife working slices from a red apple.

"Amelia, what would you say if I retired from the Return business and went in to run my Father's firm?"

Amelia chewed thoughtfully, swallowed, and said, "I thought you wanted to help Returns find peace."

"Not a lot of money in it."

"Have you seen what you pay me? Trust me, I know. But I didn't take the job because I needed money. My parents left me with enough to get by. I took it because I believe in what we're doing. I thought you did, too."

Sam took an apple slice between his teeth. "I do. I just... I thought it would be a little more lucrative is all. At this rate I'll be pushing forty before..."

"Before what, Sam?"

"It's been a few years since we all came back from the War. I know I came back later than most, but I look around and everyone is starting a career, buying a house, getting married, having children." Sam stood up and threw the apple core into the meadow. "A few spooks looking for us to call their mothers aren't exactly putting us on the fast track to any of those things."

Amelia's countenance changed, a spring of melancholy seemed to bubble up behind her striking features. "And why do you say that?" She uttered the words diplomatically.

Sam wished he could read Amelia's mind. He felt his heart racing. Did Amelia want an 'us'? Or did she not see the need for a man to establish himself before taking on the responsibility of someone else? He patted the black velvet box in his pocket, and remembered his mother's words.

Amelia looked up at him, ignoring or not seeing him nervously pat his pants pocket. Sam opened his mouth, but hesitated. "I just," he finally said, "I need to make sure everything is taken care of first, you know?"

"I suppose you have to decide what's important to you. We all do."

Sam nodded and chewed his final slice of apple. His eyes were distant. He looked to Amelia, melancholy but with his mouth closed, fixedly chewing the fruit.

Standing, Amelia brushed off her dress and held out a hand to Sam, inviting him up. "Let's walk the trail a bit more. It's been a whirlwind few days."

Taking her hand, Sam popped up and stared at her for a few moments before smiling. "Thanks, Amelia. I just need to lock up the picnic basket and leftover food in the trunk. Don't want to attract any wayward bears."

CHAPTER TEN

Charles Cox sat at the base of a great Elm tree, deep within Wright Park. Darkness had long fallen, and he could feel the ground's coldness as it wicked away the warmth of his legs and behind. Numbness had settled on his lower extremities. He'd been sitting in the same position for so long, aware that the two men standing before him grew more and more impatient with each passing minute.

A sympathetic, yet forceful stage whisper came from the larger of the two men. The voice cut through the night toward Cox. "This is way it must be," Dimitry said in his accented voice.

It was unusual for the big man to do the talking, but Leonard, who had been introduced to Cox through Gayle, was barely able to breathe through his broken and bandaged nose. Let alone speak.

Cox lifted his right hand from his knee. The gun felt so heavy. He raised it with a quaking arm, and dropped the weapon again to his lap. "I can be useful," he said, desperation in his voice. "Rockwell isn't the first rich guy I've discovered. Not even the first one that's died. Though I'm sure Gayle didn't mean to..." he trailed off. "Isn't there some other way?"

"No," Leonard spat at Cox. "Der 'sn't." He coughed from the effort. The larger man raised a hand to keep his rail thin partner from speaking further.

"Charles," Dimitry said, crouching down so as to be nearly eye to eye with him. "Is not about finding rich man, getting money for cause. You stumble on something much bigger and more important to USSR. But, you have made mess. You give away name of Gayle. You maybe connect murder to us. This can threaten our cover. Already I have to go to Working Man to tie up the loose ends. I should not be in such a place. You understand this."

Dimitry tasseled Cox's hair, his hand palming the smaller man's skull, petting him like a dog. "Now, you say you want to be useful? Because of all these reasons I give, you be useful. Follow plan and Rockwell detective no more will be on case. Detective Clemons will be laughing stock and no one will look for us. For all these reasons, you must fix now. Frank Rockwell funeral tomorrow. Fix now."

"Or," Leonard said through grinding teeth, "we'll fix it for you."

"Better if you do, no?" Dimitry said. "Is how I would die. By my own hand. Is strong death for glorious cause."

Cox again raised the quivering pistol and pressed its barrel against his temple. He squeezed his eyes tightly shut.

"Wait," Dimitry said. Cox dropped the weapon, a wave of relief surging over him like a tsunami. He couldn't keep back the tears.

"Good," Dimitry said, "you cry. Make more convincing." He pointed to the suicide note Cox held in his other hand. He had written it earlier in Dimitry's hotel room, carefully worded according to Leonard's exacting specifications.

"Put note in pocket," Dimitry said, looking to the heavens. "Perhaps will rain tonight. Ink will run. Police will check pockets when find you, don't worry."

The big Russian stood again and stepped back. Far enough away, Cox imagined, to avoid having his blood splatter across his clothing. But Cox found himself unable to bring the pistol to his head. Leonard's half-gasped demands to hurry up seemed faint and distant.

The thin man took Cox's arm roughly and forced him to press the weapon against his own head. Cox offered no resistance. He stared into the miry pools of hate that were Leonard's eyes as the thin man's bony fingers forced him to pull the trigger.

A POP sounded throughout the park, echoing off trees and dissipating into the night sky. Dimitry and Leonard stood and listened, hearing only the rustle of the squirrels overhead, disturbed by the sudden noise. Though the gunshot would likely scare off any troublesome night walkers out for a stroll, the park's location in the middle of the city made it likely that the police would soon arrive to investigate.

The two men set off at a brisk pace, not bothering to take a second look to verify that Cox was dead. There was no need.

Leonard took nearly twice as many steps to keep up with the larger man. He wheezed from the effort. "I hope none of dat got on my suit."

"You can change at hotel," Dimitry answered flatly. "Tomorrow send post card. Use code for Kremlin. Tell them atomic plans soon is ours. This is, how you say, big break. We take bourgeois money, but find he has far greater asset. Now, we just find which Rockwell has it."

"I'm betting on the son," Leonard said, raising his hand to his broken nose. "So let's find him and take it right now."

Dimitry sighed. "He will not have document on him. Besides, until police find note, they will be too near to him. But you are right. The son will know where to find plans."

"So we grab him and make him talk, the hard way?" A yellow gleam of sadism streaked across Leonard's eyes.

"No more messes," Dimitry said. "I need to keep cover. I have plan. He will bring secrets to us."

Temperatures had soared during the month of July. Frank's burial was held in the late morning, but dark suits and dresses were already adhering to perspiring backs by the time Reverend Barnaby stood to speak. Sam could feel the sweat attempting to flood down his face if it breached the levy that was the band of his hat.

"I am the resurrection and the life," Barnaby began. "He that believeth in me, though he were dead, yet shall he live: And whosoever liveth and believeth in me shall never die."

A rush of wind conjured from a bevy of program cards converted into fans, answered in reply to the Scripture reading. An eager Deacon somewhere in the rear of the crowd followed with a spirited "Amen!"

"Let us bow our hearts in prayer," Barnaby said, his black suit radiating heat, though he showed no discomfort. Sam removed his hat and feebly dabbed at the deluge with a handkerchief.

"With broken hearts and questions unanswered we come before you, our heavenly Father. We ask for grace and comfort in the wake of the loss of Frank Rockwell. We remember the one we love who is now gone from our sight. And, presumably, will stay gone this time. Father, hear our prayer..."

"Hear our prayer," answered the congregation.

Sam blinked in the heat and felt his mind begin to wander. He didn't attempt to refocus it, opting instead to observe the mood and pallor of those around him. Their eyes were closed, so he probably wouldn't have a better chance. Were any of them grieving as the Reverend described? It didn't look that way. Barnaby's face was solemn and his eyes were shut tightly in concentration as his lips continued the prayer. His mother was fanning herself furiously. She wore a look of pained acceptance. Not over the burial. She wanted to be done and out of the heat. The look she wore was the same she would give to him and Elijah as boys when they would spend too much time deliberating over a promised piece of candy at the drugstore. Hurry and pick something so we can go home, dears.

It was much the same among the remaining crowd of faces. Business associates, employees, distant relations, bowling partners, and church members seeking to support Alice all held the same disinterested expression on their faces. As if someone had extended an invitation to a doggy obedience school graduation. Funerals had become unpleasant formalities for someone they'd see soon enough again. Too soon, for some.

Amelia was an exception. She seemed to be speaking silently to herself through the ponderously long prayer, her dimples appearing and disappearing like small flashes of lighting as she moved her rosy lips in earnest oblations. Sam's heart swelled at the sight of her, and he questioned, not for the first time, his decision not to propose marriage at the mountain. She hadn't spoken much to him since the picnic, preferring to keep conversation with his mother. Sam was beginning to feel awkward around her, and he hated it.

He spied Lieutenant Clemons standing off beneath the shade of an oak tree. Something about the way Clemons was staring smoking holes into him made Sam feel uneasy. He bowed his head again, giving thanks when the Reverend ended his prayer soon after.

Detective Clemons wore a bulldog frown on his face as Sam joined him beneath the shade of the tree. A trail of ants worked their way in lines moving up and down the tree bark, just behind Clemons' back.

Sam was ready to make his pitch for helping with the case. "Thanks for coming to pay your respects."

"I don't have any respects to pay," Clemons said. Sam tilted his head, inviting further explanation. "I got word, final word, that your father had no access to anyone or anything remotely resembling government secrets. The two of you had me on a trip for biscuits and now I'm the laughing stock down at the station for it."

"That's not possible. He was sent back—"

"The hell it's not possible. I got it straight from Hoover's men. Right after I asked if he might be a spy working with two communists matching the description you gave me." Clemons poked Sam hard in the chest. "That provided me with another wonderful opportunity to be laughed at." He sent a backward kick into the tree behind him.

Sam shoved his hands in his pockets. "I'm sure there's more to it." He snapped his fingers. "We found his killer. We found her and so his case is done. He's gone back up, but we can still—"

"He comes, he goes. He comes back, and he's gone again. Each time he's snowballing whoever is upstairs to get a little more time back down here. He wanted to make a big deal for himself, one final hurrah at the expense of me and my career. I got a family to support. If that selfish crumb were here right now I'd walk right through him and spit on his grave."

"But the two communists at the bar—"

"Stop it right now, Rockwell," the Lieutenant said, squaring himself challengingly near. "I don't believe any of that for a moment. Here's the way I see it; your old man lies to the angels upstairs. They send him back. You, the dinner theater detective, come up from bumbling in Los Angeles thinking you can do my job. The Old Man comes back and springs the whole atomic secrets nonsense on me at his firm. He fills you in on the deal at Cox's place and then you go find yourself a bar and start busting up the joint, making up two goons to cover your tracks while your father does God knows what. Is that about it?"

"No," Sam said, slapping the side of the tree. He shook his head at how things were playing out. "Detective Clemons, I didn't make up what happened at that tavern. There are dangerous men on the loose, looking for whatever secrets my father had."

Clemons bumped his chest into Sam and pointed a finger at him. "Enough. Not another word. I'm not going to arrest you or bring you in for pulling the wool over my eyes. As much as I'd love to throw you behind bars for this, I'm not going to have a judge added to the chorus of people laughing at me when he dismisses your assault charges for lack of evidence. But, God help me, you listen to me; you're through as a detective, Returns or otherwise. I personally called a friend with the LAPD, and you will never work anything resembling a real case down there again. And if you intend to stay in Tacoma, I'd better not here from you unless you're bleeding out from a robbery at Daddy's firm."

The Lieutenant left Sam standing beneath the tree, pausing to stare daggers at Frank's casket as it lowered into the earth. Sam was surprised the detective didn't spit as he passed by.

The funeral, burial, and memorial service had demanded Alice's attention the entire day. She couldn't remember the last time she'd shaken so many hands nor had so many people grip her shoulder while offering a solemn nod and respectful frown. The universal gesture of empathizing grief, she called it.

All of it had been taken in stride. Alice wore a warm smile and offered thanks and conciliation about Frank until her cheeks were sore. She had to force the muscles to obey by strength of will.

She collapsed into her living room reading chair and felt the desire to kick off her shoes and put her feet up on the coffee table as Frank sometimes did. She never did like that habit of his, and the presence of Sam and Amelia demanded a more proper presentation than such a boorish show of self-indulgence. Still, she was tired, and crossed her legs at the ankle instead of at her thighs as a sort of middle ground.

Amelia sat next to Alice in Frank's old chair, picking up an issue of Look that had been inadvertently knocked to the floor. Alice patted Amelia's hand and gave her thanks with a smile.

Somewhere in the backyard, Sam was cooking steaks.

"Do you really think," Amelia said, "that you won't miss your husband at all?"

"Maybe I'll need some time to adjust to being in the house alone," Alice said, leaning her head back into the lush upholstery. It was like reclining in a cloud, and she felt an urge to sleep. "But I'll do all right. I understand that you live alone and seem to do just fine."

Amelia fidgeted. "Yes, a place in the city my parents left for me when they died. But I didn't mean to ask if you thought you'd be lonely for a while. I meant will you miss him being in your life every day?"

Alice bent herself toward Amelia, taking her hand again. "Do you still miss your parents?"

"Very much so. I wished so hard when they died that they'd come back as Returns. Come and help me know what to do next. I never had anyone else beside them, you understand."

"You poor girl," Alice said, squeezing Amelia's fingers in her hand. "I can certainly understand why you'd feel that way. But that's still different. You needed your parents. Frank and I, well, our lives had become a routine. It was like when you stop in at a service station and the attendant jumps out and starts wiping down your windshield and checking your tires. Automatic, you see."

Amelia nodded, though she didn't quite comprehend what Alice was saying. Something in her face must have told Alice as much, so she continued.

"Frank needed me to be his attendant. He'd show up hungry for pot roast, and I'd feed him. He'd get angry and start yelling, and I'd listen and try to calm him. For the past twenty-five years my life has revolved around his wants and needs, while his life revolved around—"

"His wants and needs," Amelia said, finishing the sentence for her. She cast her eyes downward, a creeping melancholy whispering in her ear. Wasn't it the same with Sam? Keeping her waiting while he attended to what he first wanted?

Alice seemed to sense this is as well. "I will say this. If Frank had died the first few years of our marriage, I would have missed him terribly. I started missing that Frank before he died."

Amelia seemed to revive at this. "Doesn't that make at least part of you feel bad he died?"

Alice waved a hand. "We all die, Amelia."

Rubbing her chin with her wrist, Amelia picked up the magazine and began to flip through its pages. "I know that, but I still don't see why we have to be so accepting of it. So what if it happens to everyone?" She put the magazine down and crossed her arms. "I hate that something as wonderful as life is yoked to something so terrible as death. That's why I agreed to work with Sam. It's bad enough that people die, but to Return and have no one ready to help? Dreadful."

"Return or not, we'll see them again," Alice said, repeating a platitude she'd heard several times throughout the day.

The savory odor of grilled steaks filled the air as Sam made his way through the back door. He placed a serving plate piled high with porterhouse in the middle of the dining room table. "I figure you ladies can cut off what you'd like. I'll take the rest."

Amelia rose, leaving Alice in her seat. "That smells wonderful, Samuel," said Alice, barely moving her head, "but I don't think anything is going to remove me from this chair."

From the front picture window Sam watched a well-groomed man, about middle age, approach. "Too bad. Mr. Turner from across the street is coming by with a bouquet of flowers. Knowing him, they're probably not for me."

Alice was up in an instant. "Oh, for heaven's sake. Frank's been in the ground for less than twenty-four hours."

Amelia looked to Sam, perplexed. "Mr. Turner," Sam told her, "is one of the many men whose hearts could love no one but my sweet mother."

Alice patted her son on the arm en route to the door. "You're sweet."

"You think he's coming here to ask your mother on a date?" said Amelia, slightly teasing Alice.

"Could be," Sam said, catching on. "She's on the market now and it wouldn't be the first time he asked her out. He did once already while Elijah and I were kids. When Dad found out he almost went over and gave him a piece of his mind. Almost. Dad wasn't a fighter, but he hated him."

"That's why he insisted on you and Elijah taking boxing lessons," Alice said from the door. "Now hush up, he's almost here."

Turner walked up the steps just as Alice opened the door. He handed her the bouquet and said, "My condolences." He didn't sound like he meant it.

"Thank you," said Alice, "but I'll see him again."

"I was wondering—"

Alice cut his sentence off by slowly closing the door. Turner frowned through the tightening sliver of an opening between him and Alice. "We're having dinner," she said before disappearing completely from Turner's view.

The door shut with a click, and then reopened. Alice popped her head out and said, "I'll go put these in water. Thanks again for thinking of Frank."

"You see," said Amelia, once Alice returned to the table. "If you didn't miss your husband you would have listened to what that poor man had to say."

"That's just Mr. Turner." Alice glanced through her lace curtains as the man walked back across the street. "Send Clark Gable over carrying flowers and see what happens." She sat at the dining table to join her son and Amelia. "I've gotten my appetite back."

Stabbing the largest steak on the serving plate, Alice began to carve it. Sam had cooked the prize to his own culinary specifications, and couldn't hide his disappointment at the loss. Alice pretended not to notice. "Tell me how the two of you met. I've never heard the entire story, only that Sam came to your aid?"

"Perhaps my finest hour," Sam said, putting a forkful of steak, pink and juicy, in his mouth.

Amelia grinned. "I was walking in Griffith Park, near the fountain, when two men started yelling the most awful things at me."

"Sailors," Sam said between chews.

"I suppose they'd been yelling at all the girls that day and I was just the most recent one to walk by. I figured they were intoxicated, so I did my best to ignore them and hurry on. But they wouldn't be quiet and started to follow me around the fountain."

"Terrible," said Alice, shaking her head. "Their mothers would be ashamed."

"Here comes the good part," Sam said, raising his eyebrows for emphasis.

"I began to worry, and started walking faster—almost a run, really. The names and invitations didn't stop, and I turned to see that they were trying to catch up with me. Well, they saw me looking and broke into a jog. I panicked and ran smack into Sam's chest. He took me by my shoulders to keep me from falling and asked," Amelia deepened her voice, 'What's the trouble, Miss?'"

"I figured it out pretty quickly," Sam interjected. "I heard the cat-calls first, and then the crumbs were standing a few feet away from us."

"Sam put himself in front of me," Amelia added.

"Right," said Sam, he and Amelia were animated, eager to tell the story together. "I figured she'd want to have something between her and these two men. They were acting like it had been too long between ports of call."

"But instead—"

"But instead, Amelia stands right beside me and says—"

"I called them disgusting beasts and told them they ought to be ashamed of themselves."

Sam broke into laughter at the memory, Amelia swiftly following.

"Good for you," said Alice, her attention rapt on the tale.

"Well, they weren't remorseful," Sam said, "They asked who was going to make them, so I—"

"So he walks right up to them—he's so much taller than most people. He made these two look like children. Then Sam grabbed each one by the collar." Amelia clenched both fists in the air to simulate the grip, her nail polish shining. "I could see how frightened of him they were. They looked shocked. Then Sam says—"

Sam rose to act out the scene. He held in each hand an invisible man, staring from left to right at their imaginary faces. "I said, 'Apologize to the lady, or I'll toss you both into the fountain.'"

Alice leaned forward. "And did you?"

"All of a sudden," Amelia said, "they found their courage. Each one grabbed one of Sam's arms."

She rose and took hold of Sam's arm, playing the role of one of the sailors.

"They were trying to get loose," said Sam, "but I wouldn't let them. So the seamen said—"

"'We're used to the water, you gorilla,'" Amelia jumped in, deepening her voice and giving it an indistinguishable accent. "'We'll take you right in with us.'"

Sam stepped up onto his chair, his head just inches below the ceiling. "So I climb up the base of the fountain and," he dropped down to the floor, Amelia still holding his arm, "jumped right into the fountain."

"Samuel!" Alice exclaimed. Amelia burst into another fit of laughter.

"His shoes on and everything," Amelia giggled out, she had let go of Sam's arm and was gingerly holding her side as she laughed, "He said, 'Well, now I'm used to the water, too. So how about it? Are you going to apologize or do I have to pull you in with me?'"

"And," Sam said lightly, "they apologized."

"But you were the one who was all wet," said Alice.

"Not exactly," Sam answered. He locked eyes with Amelia. "I may have accidentally pulled them in when I used their shirt collars to help myself out of the fountain. I escorted Amelia home and left those sharks spluttering in their natural environment."

Alice watched the couple intently.

"Once he found out where I lived," Amelia said, "He just kept happening to walk through the neighborhood on his way to work. When he found out how interested I was in Returns, he offered me a job, and the rest is history."

Alice smiled warmly. "That beats how Frank and I first met. I caught him staring at me at church, he still went back then, and each week that followed I'd find a flower waiting for me in the pew." She inclined her head, recalling long past years. "Just a flower. No card or note. My first and only secret admirer. Frank must have realized how much it irked Daddy, because he didn't fess up to being the admirer for nearly two months. Three months after that, we were married."

"My but that's romantic," Amelia said. She was earnest as

ever. Given Frank's outbursts two nights ago, she never would have guessed the ghost to have once been a Romeo. Delight for Alice's memory shone without blemish in her gleaming smile.

The look of remembrance lingered on Alice's face. "Yes," she said, seeming to drift off into the distant seas of her memory, "I suppose it was."

"Are you talking about my father?" Sam asked.

"He was different then, Samuel. Just about all he had to offer was love." She gave a devilish smile. "And those dark eyes."

That his father once wooed his mother with all of the trappings of a lovesick puppy was a revelation. Sam's head buzzed. The only time he recalled his father giving flowers to Alice was on anniversaries. The week before another year of marriage passed, Frank would make an announcement for all in earshot, generally Sam, Alice, and Elijah. "I've ordered you flowers for our anniversary, Alice. I trust you'll find them satisfactory. Let no one say that Frank Rockwell doesn't know his duty!"

The Frank Rockwell Sam knew made big shows of duty, not love. Sam always assumed his father proposed with a ring in one hand and a memo detailing the ways in which he would be a dutiful and effective provider in the other. A smart union that would mutually assure a successful future posterity for them and any future children heretofore unnamed.

A secret admirer? Leaving flowers for the girl he loved? Sam mulled over this new side of the man who considered financial success a prerequisite to inviting someone to share life with you. "Master yourself," he would say, "and then you may master your domestic domain."

"What time are you taking Amelia to the airport tomorrow?"

Alice's question shattered Sam's thoughts like a baseball through a window.

Shaking his head, Sam glanced at Amelia. "Early. With the roosters."

Alice rose from her chair, the others rising as well. She turned to Amelia, embracing her. "I'm sorry I won't be able to see you off at the airport, but it's Sunday and I don't want to miss the service, especially with all Reverend Barnaby has done for me this week."

"Thank you, Mrs. Rockwell."

Alice climbed a few steps before turning to say, "Please, call me Alice." She gave an exaggerated nod, and looking directly at her son, said, "You probably would like some time to talk, just the two of you. I feel tired enough to crawl right into bed as it is. Goodnight."

Sam and Amelia sat close on the sofa. For all her attempts at conversation, Amelia didn't feel like she was getting through. Sam seemed distracted and, at times, forlorn. She supposed it was all right, she hadn't exactly been talkative after their trip to the mountain, it's just that she expected... more from the trip and couldn't hide her disappointment.

"I've noticed that you stopped talking like a dime-store detective," Amelia said.

After a pause, Sam said, "Yeah, turns out that whole act withers under the light of an actual detective."

"Well, I like the real you much better."

"Thanks."

Sam shifted forward on the couch, resting his elbows atop his knees. He held his chin up on interwoven fingers, his brows creased.

"What's bothering you, Sam?" Amelia asked, leaning forward and repositioning herself to see Sam's face.

"Amelia, I—" he cut himself off. His voice sounded nervous and uneven. He drew a breath and began again. "I don't think I'll be following you to Los Angeles. Not anytime soon." He could see Amelia's scrutiny from the corners of his vision. He couldn't bring himself to meet her eyes.

Looking forward, he tried to explain. "My father and I caused a lot of trouble for Lieutenant Clemons. We nearly cost him his job, I think. Whether he was mistaken or made it all up, I don't know, but my father didn't have any dossier of atomic secrets."

Amelia gave a start. "That sounds bad."

"It is. Clemons made a fool of himself because of it. Compound that with the fact that I let him believe I was a trained detective, and you can see why I'm in his dog house."

"That sounds like a reason to leave for Los Angeles sooner."

"It's no good. He made calls to contacts in the LAPD to blacklist me. And, from what an old army buddy I had check up on the office says, our place of business has already been turned back into a supply closet. That's my fault though; I was pretty behind on the rent."

"Los Angeles is a big place," Amelia said, trying to keep an encouraging pep in her voice. She didn't like where the conversation seemed to be going. "You can find new opportunities in another part of the city."

Sam let his body fall into the back of the sofa. "About the only opportunity I have left is taking over for my father at Rockwell Fiduciary. Assuming I don't make a mess of that, too. I know as much about finances as I do detective work."

Amelia stood and wrung her hands. Fighting an internal war over what to say next. "Sam, I need you to tell me exactly what you're thinking. I just can't figure us out."

"I'm sorry. I need to stay up here for a while and work to get some capital. If business is good, I can see about expanding to Los Angeles or even have someone run the place up here while I head back down to get things going again."

"Sam, if this is about making enough money—"

"It's not just the money. I need to know I can take care of you."

"We can take care of us," Amelia said, taking a step toward him.

"Maybe. I don't know. What about kids and everything? I have to be sure that everything is good. A man shouldn't jump into these things blindly."

Amelia folded her arms tightly, hugging herself. She walked a few steps away from Sam and stopped on the other side of the coffee table. "How long will that take?"

Sam stood up.

"You know what, never mind that. What about the Returns?" Amelia asked, her voice pleading. "I thought you wanted to help people. If you really can't do it in Los Angeles, then help them here."

"I want to ask you to stay, Amelia. It's all I want. And I do want to help Returns. I just..." He ran his fingers into his hair and pulled down tightly. "I don't know how to do any of these things until my life gets squared away. I have to be a good provider,

Amelia. If my father taught me anything, it was that."

Amelia stared at her fingers as they worked themselves over one another. She nodded, fighting hard against the tears welling in her eyes. She stood, straightened herself, and slowly made her way upstairs.

Sam fought against the urge to kick over the coffee table. How had things gotten to this point? He watched Amelia slowly ascend the staircase. This was the time when Cary Grant would rush after her, grab hold and spin her around and kiss her while the music rose in crescendo and weepy dates would lean their heads against their beau's shoulder. He let out a helpless sigh.

"I'm sorry, Amelia," he called after her.

She didn't reply.

CHAPTER ELEVEN

It had been two weeks since Amelia's conversation with Sam, but she rarely went more than a few hours without thinking about it. Life seemed to be in a holding pattern. She was out of work, but hadn't spent much time looking for another job. She took on with Sam to help Returns, not to grow her bank account. There was always a high demand for young women in Los Angeles, but the papers never mentioned Returns, and she wasn't interested in much of anything else.

Perhaps she would see about going back to school to become a nurse. Maybe work in a nursing home. Or maybe Sam... she shook away the nascent thought.

Carrying a paper bag filled with the week's groceries, she looked both ways before slowly crossing to her home. She reached the front stoop and paused, looking up and down the palm-lined city sidewalk. It was habit, a hopeful search for Sam. Amelia felt a surge of giddy anticipation that he might once again 'just happen' to walk down her street. Amelia had grown to adore Sam for his overt forms of subtlety.

She steeled herself with a thin smile. He wasn't in Los Angeles, she knew. He hadn't left Tacoma and wouldn't be happening by, no matter how much she hoped. Balancing the grocery bag on her hip, she unlocked the door.

Sam, she thought. How do you abide someone who says they're crazy about you, but won't actually back those words up? She shut the door with a heel kick, more vicious than she intended. Some of her frustration escaped with the blow.

At the kitchen counter, Amelia pulled bananas from the brown paper bag. She placed the fruit next to an unfinished letter for Sam explaining that she wasn't able to retrieve any personal effects from his apartment, which already had a new tenant. The office was cleaned out too, but he already knew that. She meant to mail the letter days earlier, but she couldn't decide how to end it. Would she write Sam goodbye for now or goodbye forever? Her answer depended on the day.

An urgent, rapid knock jitterbugged down the hall from the front door. Amelia's heart jumped at the thought of Sam standing on the porch, hat in hand. It was a goodbye-for-now sort of day. She walked quickly to the knocking, wiping her hands as she went.

Turning open the door, the outside sunlight was nearly eclipsed by the biggest beast of a man Amelia had ever seen. He wore his blond hair in flat top, and his shoulders were nearly as wide as the door frame. In front of him was a thin, diminutive man that Amelia took an immediate disliking to, though he hadn't spoken a word. The little man picked incessantly at his coat sleeves and wore a heavy bandage across his nose, skin still purple near his eyes from whatever had broken it.

"May I help you?" Amelia said through a small opening in the door, just large enough to frame her face. Then, it dawned on her who these men were. Sam had vividly described his fight with them in that tavern. Hopefully she could play dumb until they left and call Sam. Her heart raced, but her face betrayed no fear.

"You're Rockwell's girl," Leonard, the thin man said.

"Who?" Amelia asked, surreptitiously attempting to close the door. It wouldn't budge. She glanced up and saw the large man— had Sam said Dimitry?—gripping the door with his colossal hand. He could force it open at will, she knew.

"I wasn't asking," said Leonard. He produced a snub nosed pistol through sleight of hand, picking at a piece of lint that somehow turned into a gun. The thin man motioned for her to step back, following her into the house. The burly Russian gently closed the door behind them.

"What do you want with me and why are you forcing your way into my home?" Her face felt hot. How dare these men come to her home and threaten her. "I'm sorry Sam did such a number on you, but I'm hardly to blame for that am I?" Amelia couldn't help herself. It wasn't the right thing to say, but these two hooligans deserved some sort of reproach.

The Russian scowled and Leonard's eyes grew hot with anger.

"Do you have it or not?" the thin man asked.

"Have what?"

Big Dimitry stepped forward, his Russian accent menacing. "We are wanting to have atomic plans now."

"W-what?" This was not what she expected. A threat or message for Sam, maybe. But not this. But then, why else would they be in Los Angeles? "I think there's some sort of mistake-"

"Zip it, dolly," Leonard said, jabbing the pistol toward her. "There's no mistake. You thought you could throw us by splitting up. Well, it's not going to work."

Amelia began to tremble. "I-I don't have anything like what you're asking for."

The thin man narrowed his eyes. "I've got ways to know if you're telling the truth, girl."

Captain Buford sat on a smooth stone bench looking at his boot's reflection in the marble floor when Frank abruptly appeared before him, yelling as if in mid-sentence.

"-good provider!" Frank shouted. His voice was high and aggravated. He gave a jolt, as if suddenly doused with icy water at the busy halls of the Pearly Gates Administration Building.

The old Confederate's enchantment with the mirror like polish of his boots gave way to a curiosity at Frank's abrupt Recall. Buford stroked his beard, forever oiled and trimmed, and frowned. "Mr. Rockwell?"

"Oh," Frank said, noticing the Confederate for the first time. "Hello, Stonewall."

"You mistake me for my better, sir."

Frank waved his hand dismissively, batting away the words.

"Gone for two weeks," Buford purred in Dixie. "A rather significant Return trip. It sounds as though you were recalled in the middle of something important."

"What do you mean 'two weeks?' It's barely been a day."

"Held in limbo then, I wonder?"

Frank began looking over heads, searching for someone. "Where's that Eamon fellow located? I don't see how anyone expects me to save the United States from the Soviet menace when they're popping me in and out of heaven's rest stop every other day."

Holding an arm out to invite Frank to walk with him, Buford marched with military precision down the hall. Frank followed suit. "Time," Buford called back, "does not always work between living and dead here as you think it may. I know where Eamon's office is. I've had more than enough time to know where everything is around here. I wouldn't mind being put in limbo until the last day. It's been so long."

The Captain led the way, but stopped, chewing his lip as he turned to face Frank. "Permit me to say, from experience-"

"Go on."

"Obliged. I have observed that being sent down, Returning, is relatively common in this epoch of history. Your Second World War seems to have impacted heaven and earth. But most souls Return once and move on. Getting recalled and Returning a second time, as you did, is extremely rare. To be recalled still a third time, as you again just have, and Return again is, literally, unheard of. I fear you're here for good."

"Stuff and nonsense, Johnny Reb." Buford emitted a chuckle at the name.

Frank halted. "I'm sorry. I'm... out of sorts. I need to find a way back home." He shoved his hands in his pockets and kicked at the marble floors. "I need to see my wife again. Here you are trying to help me and... I'm afraid I don't even recall your name, Captain..."

"Jeremiah Buford." The Confederate nodded and pointed with a white-gloved hand. "And it looks like Mr. Eamon has come out to meet you."

The angel walked purposefully from an open doorway that led to the main hall. Eamon's slick black hair, parted and shining from pomade, reflected the light from massive crystal chandeliers hanging high overhead. A woman wearing a black dress followed. Eyes fixed intently on Frank, she emoted scorn beneath her short bangs. Eamon seemed to take no notice of Frank or the Captain, instead turning to speak with the woman.

His inattention did not sit well with Frank. "Well?" he demanded.

The two stopped talking and Eamon gave Frank a once over. Any admiration Eamon once held for Frank was noticeably absent. "Rockwell," Eamon said. There was contempt in his voice. He pointed a finger accusingly at Frank. "A fine mess of things your cock and bull story has made. Saving the world, what? I'll be blessed if I can save my bloody job after letting you go back. Your clerk has been demoted to an elevator bellhop, not that you'll care. The poor chap nearly had kittens when he found out. As for me, I spent the better part of two hundred years to reach my situation and you'll have me out of it in forty-eight hours."

"Come off it," Frank said, playing up his business instincts. "I did you a favor. Imagine what might have happened if you hadn't sent me back. Now fix this mess and let me on my way back down."

"You certainly didn't do me any favors," said the woman, giving Frank an icy enough stare to require a dog team to deliver it.

"Quite," said Eamon.

"What's it to you?" Frank asked the woman.

"I suppose you hadn't seen her, had you?" said Eamon. "This is Gayle Shore, your murderer."

"You mean I really was killed by a woman? This is outrageous!" shouted Frank. He turned to Gayle. "How dare you? I was in the prime of life, a beautiful flower of the field, plucked short by the greedy hands of a passerby."

"Don't snap your cap," said Gayle. "It was an accident."

"A likely story," answered Frank. "Eamon! I demand she be punished."

Eamon let out an exasperated sigh while Captain Buford rumbled with small, deep-throated chuckles.

"I think I've been punished enough already," snapped Gayle. "It's thanks to you that I'm here already. I planned on repenting in a few decades once I had some grandchildren, but I suppose that won't happen now thanks to your delusions of grandeur."

"I don't know what you're talking about."

Eamon sighed anew and scratched his pencil-thin mustache. "Please, enough! I called her in merely to acquire as much information on the mess you've created as possible. She's on her way to processing. You should be too, Mr. Rockwell. There'll be no more Returns for you."

"But the atomic secrets!" Frank protested.

A look of disdain flooded Eamon's features. He looked like an irate Errol Flynn, ready to cross swords. "That will do, Mr. Rockwell."

Captain Buford clapped Frank's shoulder solemnly. Frank searched the Confederate's face for some sign of hope, but saw only a sympathetic knowing. This was it, then. Frank would have to be processed again. If they didn't send him up he'd probably spend the next hundred years with Buford. He was sure he wouldn't be sent down like the murderous Gayle. She tapped her fingers impatiently against folded arms and would not look in Frank's direction.

"It's the same up here as it is on earth," said Frank, "no one cares a hoot about what happened to Frank Rockwell." He looked glumly at the ground.

Gayle rolled her eyes and addressed Eamon. "I think you're making a mistake in not sending me back. I knew the men who killed me, they won't stop until—"

Eamon interrupted the woman's pleading. "We've been over this. I've had my fill of speculative Returns. If something happens before you've been processed, we'll see." He gripped Gayle's shoulder and smiled as he gave it a squeeze.

A red-jacketed courier walked straight to Eamon, handing him a sealed piece of folded paper. Eamon examined the crest on the seal and frowned. He opened the missive with his thumb and began to read while the courier waited. Eamon dropped the hand holding the letter to his side and to the messenger said, "And you're quite sure this is accurate?"

"Got it direct from a guardian on the scene, boss."

"Dash it all," said Eamon. His voice conveyed the weight

resting on his shoulders. "Very well. Tell control I'll handle the situation personally."

The courier clicked his shoes, turned, and was off down the expansive hall.

All eyes were on Eamon as he stuffed the paper into his front pocket. The angel looked to Gayle, then to Frank. "It seems that your ruse requires all of us, save Captain Buford, to Return once more."

"A ruse? How dare you," Frank said, spinning an index finger in the air.

The trio disappeared, leaving Buford alone. He slumped his shoulders and stared up to the vaulted ceiling, gilded and twinkling. "Unbelievable."

Tight cords bound Amelia's wrists together. She sat in the back seat, cramped and uncomfortable. Leonard forced her into the car when the sun still shone overhead. The daylight faded, she could see her captors only through the glare of oncoming headlights, which grew less and less frequent as the miles piled on.

"Last chance to take a leak," Leonard, the thin man, said. Driving the vehicle, he leered at her through the rear-view mirror.

Amelia curled her lip in disgust. The thin man probably couldn't see her, but such crudeness should not go unashamed. "You're disgusting."

Leonard seemed to crawl in his seat, accelerating. Amelia fell against the back of the leather bench from the sudden change in speed. Big Dimitry grunted a singular chuckle. "You should be slowing down," he said to Leonard.

"You don't like how I drive, feel free to take a turn," the thin man answered. He had been driving non-stop from Los Angeles, except for bathroom breaks. The men took turns relieving themselves at service station restrooms while Amelia was forced to wander from desolate stretches of highway, hiding herself as best she could behind bushes while Leonard stared from the waiting vehicle. She wished Sam would have done more than break the disgusting little creature's nose.

"No, you drive," Dimitry said. "I am needing to be rested for work. You know this." He nestled himself against the passenger door, settling his head against the glass. His muscle-bound bulk leaned heavy against the door, giving Amelia visions of the steel bending outward to send the mammoth man tumbling onto the highway mid-slumber. Unfortunately, the door held.

The hum of the tires spinning on the paved road whispered lullabies to Amelia. She prayed that Sam would find her, safely, before it was too late. These men would surely kill her when she'd filled whatever purpose they needed. She fought against sleep, but her eyes grew absurdly heavy and she drifted into a restless sleep.

Fatigue crept from the back of the car, accosting Leonard soon after Amelia was out. He reached the California-Oregon border and fought hard to keep his eyes open. The town of Brookings came, and went. A road sign announced fifteen miles until Bandon, Oregon. The sign was a revelation. Leonard didn't recall putting Gold Beach behind them. He strained to remember something about passing through the town. Nothing. A sinking feeling that he slept through the trip bombarded his stomach.

The coastal highway continued to wind and dip alongside the Pacific Ocean, shining black beneath the moonlit night. Leonard felt his head nod, heavy, and jerked himself awake again. No good. He would kill everyone in the car if he kept going. He pulled to the side of the road and joined his partner and captive in slumber.

Just a couple hours, he thought. We'll still make Portland by breakfast.

Amelia woke in degrees, eyes fluttering and then squinting as the morning's light penetrated her lashes. Through fogged window glass she could see the gray morning clouds blown in from the sea. Leonard and Dimitry snored in the front seats, their necks bent at awkward angles as they slept.

For a moment, she contemplated opening the doors and running madly to escape. She would find a rock to fray the ropes around her wrists until she was untied. The dire reality of her captivity soon erased those thoughts. She didn't know where she was or how far she could flee before the two men, both untied, caught her again.

A car passed with a whoosh of air, causing her vehicle to rock slightly from its wake. Amelia couldn't run, but she could still find help. Perhaps she could signal to a passing motorist that she was in trouble. But, the fogged windows probably blocked out any hope of that.

Pressing the cords around her wrists against the steamy glass,

Amelia rubbed away the condensation. With a little luck, the dripping wet clarity might allow some passing motorist to see the trouble she was in. Lord willing, they would report her abduction to the police.

She wiped her passenger window clean, leaving only dewdrops. She heard the approach of another vehicle and pressed her bound wrists against the glass. The car didn't as much as slow down. The driver probably didn't even bother to look as he passed.

Crawling onto the rear dash, Amelia began to defog the rear window, hopeful that another motorist would better see her if looking straight on. A third car approached from the distance. Amelia heard a rustle from the front seat, and turned to see the big man adjust himself. Her attention went back to the rear window, arms working frantically until they burned.

The driver probably couldn't see her from the distance, but he soon would. Amelia pressed her snugly wrapped arms hard against the glass. She could just see the form of a vehicle grow distinct as it neared.

Just a little bit closer and the driver would see her. She recognized the black and white paint job of the car—the police! She knew her rescue was coming. Her heart jumped, and then she screamed at a sudden sharp pressure running from her ankle up to her lower calf. Instinctively she tried to kick her leg free, turning to see Dimitry's gargantuan hand as it engulfed her lower leg.

The big Russian gave a yank, and Amelia tumbled down back into her seat. She pressed herself into a corner, undaunted, and subtly raised her wrists above the window line. Dimitry's trunk-like arm shot out and pulled her hands down, pinning them tightly against her lap. She squirmed to free herself from the Russian's strength.

"No more of this," Dimitry said. Leonard stirred at his partner's words. The thin man glanced at Amelia through the mirror and then sat bolt upright. Amelia smiled inwardly. The thin man had spotted the patrol car too, then.

Leonard twirled around in his seat and looked at Amelia's restraints. The black and white police cruiser approached, reducing its speed slightly. With a metallic TING, Leonard produced a cruel-looking blade and pointed it at Amelia. "Keep your hands down or I'll put this," he waved the knife, "right in your pretty little eye." Amelia stopped fidgeting. "Dimitry, you said there wouldn't be any cops on one-oh-one."

"Usually is not," Dimitry said, shrugging a pair of shoulders that would help Atlas hold up the world just fine. "You stop too close to town."

The police car was almost to them. Leonard hissed. "Eyes forward, doll."

Amelia obeyed, her captives also facing forward as the patrol car slowed. From the corner of her eye, Amelia could see the officer examining the vehicle as he drove past.

Stop. Please, stop, she prayed.

The cruiser's light flashed. A burst of adrenaline worked through Amelia's system. She exhaled deeply as the car pulled to the shoulder in front of them.

Leonard swore and turned again to Amelia, knife in hand. "Hold out your hands," he said. When she hesitated he yelled, "Now!" She put them forward, wrists up, plaintively. "I'm going to cut you loose and you're going to keep your mouth shut, you hear me?"

Fat chance of that, Amelia thought as the cords dropped from her red wrists. "Or what, you'll kill me?"

"No," said Leonard as he gathered the fallen strands of rope. "We still need you, but we don't need him. Keep your mouth shut or Dimitry will crush that cop's head like a grape. And then his old lady will get the call that every copper's wife dreads."

The officer was out of his car and walked down the highway toward them. Amelia believed the men would murder him without a second thought. She wouldn't let herself be the cause of someone's death. Dejected, she slumped back into her seat.

"Try not to look so sad," Dimitry said, utterly casual. "Looks suspicious to policeman."

Leonard rolled down his window to prepare for the visit. He shot daggers at Amelia through the mirror as the policeman drew closer.

Reaching the window, the officer bent down and looked at the trio. "You folks all right?"

Amelia watched the officer's head bob just outside, attempting to get a complete look inside. His face was simple and his smile helpful. She felt safe by his being near, though he was in far graver danger than even she was. The violent image of Dimitry grabbing the officer's head and squeezing it between his two vise-like hands until it burst played unwelcome in her mind. Help was close, but murder closer. She did her best to not look suspicious. To keep the officer alive.

"I got sleepy late last night driving up to Portland," Leonard said. "Didn't think I could make it back into town so I pulled over here. We were just about to move on when you stopped. Thanks for checking on us."

"Portland, eh?" said the officer. He looked back at Amelia and smiled. She returned a weak smile of her own, the best she could muster. She cast her eyes downward, when the officer looked back to Leonard and Dimitry. "You fellas ought to let the lady sit up front, don't you think?"

"I no fit in back," said Dimitry. "And I not know how to drive."

"She can't either," Leonard said, showing his teeth in an apologetic smile.

The officer squinted at Dimitry and snapped his fingers. "I know you," he said. "I know you."

"Da," Dimitry said with a smile. "I hear often. I do much travel."

"Crusher Koskov!" the officer said, proud of his recall. "I've seen you a few times. I'm a big fan. All us boys at the station are." He pointed to Leonard, "Who's this?"

"My manager," Dimitry said. The officer shook the Big Russian's hand. In the back seat, Amelia wanted to cry for confusion.

"Say," the officer said. "Can I have your autograph? Name's Darryl." He handed over his pen and ticket book. Dimitry scribbled on the pad and returned the items to Officer Darryl.

"To Darryl," the officer read aloud, "Great people make America great." He looked up from the autograph. "Wow! Thanks."

"Anything for fan," Dimitry said, "We must be leaving for Portland now or we miss show. Saturday, so is on television. I think of you when I win."

Officer Darryl stood back and nodded, wearing a Cheshire grin as Leonard pulled the car onto the highway. Amelia rubbed her wrists, unsure whether she should be thankful the officer failed to notice the swollen red rings the coiled ropes made. Probably for the best. The man was still alive, his day apparently made.

No one made an effort to tie her again. Perhaps her silence had been viewed as trustworthiness. Maybe the rope was in the trunk. Amelia rode to Portland in silence, the hum of the road lulling her into a trance as she pondered Officer Darryl's reaction to Crusher Koskov, atomic secrets, and whether she'd ever see Sam again. She was sure now that he was her only hope for survival.

CHAPTER TWELVE

Sam sat twirling a silver fountain pen he'd found in his father's—his—desk drawer. The day had just begun, and Sam had no illusions it would be a productive one. It would take some time before he had a thorough enough grasp of his father's business to take day-to-day control. He felt eager to distract himself from Amelia, now back in Los Angeles. But sitting in an office idly for hours wasn't doing the trick.

Why hadn't he asked her to stay? Asked her to... Plenty of time for that later, Sam thought. Once he made something of himself he could tackle that question, if Amelia would wait for him. He shook clear the web Amelia made of his mind. He already spent half the night lying awake in bed, torturing himself with questions. That had become a trend since Amelia flew south.

The sleepless night pounced on Sam, forcing him to yawn. Keeping alert would be difficult today. All he wanted to do was to curl up beneath his desk and nap on the plush carpet.

Assuming control of Rockwell Fiduciary was the business of the day. Or at least, getting a few steps closer to it. The plan had been for Sam to shadow Clyde Harper, his father's more than capable senior employee. That plan fizzled when news trickled out about Frank's death. A string of clients called in, seeking to close their accounts and take their business elsewhere. Sam's erstwhile mentor had been on the horn nonstop for the past week convincing investors to stick with the company.

A few clients had come in wanting to meet Sam personally, but he and Mr. Harper both thought it would be wise to avoid any interactions until his face had a chance to fully heal. First impressions and all.

Harper managed to keep all the worried clients but one, and he assured Sam that particular client was financially a small fish. Sam made a mental note to ask him if he felt he deserved a raise, and then give him one whether he said yes or no. He liked the idea of handing out raises. The company could afford it. Probably.

Herbert Hoover stared at Sam from the floor. Sam thought he might put up a portrait of Abraham Lincoln or Calvin Coolidge, but instead commissioned an artist who lived in the Stadium District to paint him and his father together. That would show the family ownership line and all. It would be good for business, people with money tended to expect things like that.

Suppressing another yawn, he turned his attention to a photograph of his mother on a bureau and imagined Amelia's picture standing in its place. A gloom, like gray October rain, came over Sam. He slunk into a pitiable slouch, failing to notice the dapper, black suited Englishman who appeared at the door.

Eamon announced his presence with a quick, polite cough. The abruptness of the noise in the silent room caused Sam to jump in his chair wildly. Realizing he was not alone, Sam regained himself and flattened both palms on his desk. He offered Eamon a weak smile.

"I'm terribly sorry," said Eamon, "It was not my intent to startle you."

"It wasn't my intent to flip my wig," said Sam, smoothing down his hair. "Let's keep my high jump between you and me, and just call it exercising."

"Certainly, Mr. Rockwell."

"A man needs to keep in good physical condition. It's no good sitting at a desk all day."

"Of course," said Eamon, taking a seat before Sam.

"Fine, fine. So how did you get past the tower guard?" Sam modeled his bruised face for display. "I'm not supposed to see any clients until I regain my natural beauty."

"Don't hold it against the poor chaps. I made sure to appear directly in your office from the administration building. You see I'm an—"

"Ghost," interrupted Sam. "Sorry, pal, I'm out of that line of work. Not enough spooks out there to keep food on the table."

"I'm not a ghost, Mr. Rockwell. If I were 'an' ghost, I'd be guilty of crimes of grammar. I am an angel. One assigned to overseeing the administrative duties involving Returns."

"Should've known," Sam said, coming alongside Eamon to

take a seat on the desk. "Legitimate Returns rarely seemed to come my way."

"I should think not, what with your being unlicensed. Though you're to blame for that," Eamon muttered under his breath, just loud enough for Sam to hear.

"I had a dream about that. What do you mean unlicensed?"

"You get the dreams, that's step one. Step two is to acquire the license. Surely you don't imagine that we'd send Returns to anyone with a magnifying glass and the words 'Private Investigator' on the door?"

"Funny. Didn't stop clients from coming, though. A few, anyway."

"Many Returns take to wandering and get lost. They likely found you after a bit of looking around and," Eamon smiled apologetically, "settled."

"Swell. So did you pop in just to tell me why my career took a catastrophic nose-dive, or was there something else I can do for a pencil-pushing angel today?"

"You may call me Eamon."

"Sure, Eamon." Sam folded his arms. "Now how can I help you?"

Eamon stood and began pacing the room. "Mr. Rockwell, I need you to take up your father's case once again. Those two soviet spies you encountered are preparing to make an awful mess of things."

"Why not ask a licensed detective?"

"The nearest one is in Lebanon, Pennsylvania and we haven't the time to get him here." Eamon leaned in close to Sam. "Your help is desperately needed, but there are certain rules. I need for you to be most explicit in stating your desire to help before I can tell you anything further. I can't be seen as forcing you into working for us."

Sam rolled his eyes. "I'm glad to help. Always have been."

Eamon clapped. "Excellent. Now, I'm going to disappear and when I return, I will introduce you to someone. It might be a while. Do try to control yourself when I return."

The angel vanished.

Circling around to his telephone, Sam pulled a wrinkled, cream-colored business card from his pocket. He dialed the number, glancing up with each click of the rotary for Eamon and his guest.

Detective Clemons answered on the second ring.

"Clemons, it's Sam Rockwell... that's right... Sorry, it's an emergency, though. Someone from upstairs appeared in my office and told me... No, I did quit. I mean my new office... Right. So he says there really is trouble with my Father's death, he says those Russians—"

The receiver exploded with Clemons' impatient roar. Sam held the phone as far from his head as the cord would allow, half expecting some nearby accountant to enter and see about the commotion. Eamon might even have heard it upstairs. When the noise subsided, Sam cautiously brought the phone back to his ear.

"These are dangerous men, Lieutenant... Yes, you are too, I understand. But these men... right, I remember... Detective, are you going to help me or not because I—" The concussive wave from Clemons slamming the phone down on the other end nearly caused Sam's hair to flutter. He rolled up his sleeves and tapped his foot silently in the deep carpets.

Eamon reappeared alongside a young woman with an aquiline nose wearing a black dress. "Introductions," the angel said. He gestured to Sam. "This is Sam Rockwell."

Sam nodded his head. "Hello." The woman looked familiar, but he couldn't quite place her name or face.

Eamon gestured to the woman. "This is Gayle Shore, your father's killer."

Sam looked as if he'd just seen a horse ride a cowboy down the street, and took an involuntary step backward. He recognized her now; the deathly pallor from under the sheet was gone. She looked flush and alive. A Return.

Gayle stepped forward. "It was an accident, I swear." She reached out and touched Sam instinctively on the arm. A bitter cold cut through his bones.

"Sure," said Sam, attempting to rub warmth back into his limb. "Why, I killed two people by accident just this morning on my way to breakfast."

"Oh, but it was," said Gayle. Her face blushed red in spite of its spectral nature. She appeared to Sam contrite. He regretted the joke. "It was Charlie's idea," Gayle said.

"Charles Cox?"

"Yes. He said his boss was so rich that he'd never notice if someone took a stack or two of money from his office safe. He spent weeks trying to figure out the combination but couldn't do it. Your father would make sure everyone quit working at the same time, so Charlie never had a chance to snoop around after dark. So we came up with a plan for me to hide in the ladies room until your father went home for the night."

"Then take a look around and see if you couldn't get into that safe," said Sam, feeling like a detective again.

Gayle looked down. "Yes. I thought he had left. All the lights were off except for a desk lamp or two. I quietly crept into his office—the door was unlocked. To my surprise, I saw the safe sitting wide open. But I didn't see any money inside, just an envelope. I grabbed it, but before I had a chance to open it, I heard a toilet flush. I panicked and hid myself—"

"Behind the plants," Sam concluded.

"Y-yes," Gayle admitted.

"That's how I was able to figure out you were a she and not a he. Your heels left prints in the carpet."

"Oh," she said with indifference. Sam frowned; even Clemons had been impressed with that bit of detective work. He stayed quiet and let her continue her confession.

"I was carrying a small handbag and put the envelope inside. That's when I realized someone had put a gun there. I don't know who. Maybe Charlie trying to keep me safe."

"Nothing safer than sending your gal in to do an armed robbery for you," deadpanned Sam.

Eamon gave a cough.

"Oh, I know we're in a hurry but I just have to get this off my chest," said Gayle to Eamon. She turned back to Sam. "I thought maybe your father had the cash somewhere else, so I snuck up behind him. I meant to point the gun at his back, and tell him to hand over the money. But before I could say 'freeze', the gun went off and... and I killed him," she trailed off softly.

"Never put your finger on the trigger unless you're ready to shoot whatever you're pointing at," said Sam. "First rule of firearms."

"What?" Gayle cast Sam a squinting inspection.

"Sorry, force of habit. My old man said that to my brother and I every time we even smelled gun oil."

Eamon coughed and said, "Brother and *me*."

Sam shrugged as Gayle picked up the conversation. "I'm sorry for what I did to him."

"We'll see him again," said Sam.

"It's that sort of attitude," Eamon interjected, "that prevented us from sending more Returns in centuries past. I don't know why we send so many now, to be honest. Providence; who can know it?"

Sam leaned against the front of his deks. "So what's the plan? I'm guessing you brought her here for more than an apology."

"Right," said Eamon. "Those men you fought are scoundrels of the lowest quality."

"And thanks to your Father," Gayle said, "they murdered me."

Sam wore a puzzled look.

"When your father Returned," Eamon said, "fraudulently, I might add, he mentioned something about atomic secrets. These men are Soviet spies and believed Gayle stole those secrets. They feared a double cross and murdered her. Charles Cox was next. He didn't have a classified dossier, either."

"Why isn't Charlie part of the angel brigade?" asked Sam. Eamon stood behind Gayle and motioned his finger downward as he pantomimed a whistle. Sam took the hint. "Never mind where he is. So what do you need from me?"

"One of our men in the field overheard them discussing their next steps, confirming what Gayle told me on her arrival. They're after you, Samuel."

"So you came to warn me? Thanks." Sam went back behind the desk and pulled his father's—his—pistol. He strapped on a shoulder holster he purchased with his first paycheck. "I'll be ready."

Eamon stepped forward and raised a hand as Sam put on his coat. "I must interject here for the sake of clarification. They're after you but not directly." Eamon paused, tugging at his collar. "They've apprehended Miss Amelia Martin. They plan to use her to get the dossier from you."

Desperation stormed across Sam's dark eyes. He placed the gun, suddenly heavy, on the desk. "Oh, no."

"I know how to track them down," said Gayle. "The big one, Dimitry, keeps an unusual profession for his cover."

Sam swung open his heavy executive doors, causing the bustling outer office to freeze. Clyde Harper, employee of the year, excused himself from a phone call and rushed his way toward Sam and his ghostly entourage.

"Sorry, Clyde," Sam said. "I know I'm not supposed to show my face until it heals up. Sorry, ladies."

"Seeing that face is fine by me," called a woman from somewhere among the throng of desks.

"Give her a raise," said Sam. Then he thought of Amelia and guilt washed over him. The levity came whether he wanted it or not. "Look, I need to borrow someone's car to drive to Portland. Who can lend me one? I don't have a moment to spare."

"Oh, dear," said Harper, wringing his hands. "I'm afraid none of us drive to work. Your father insisted that all of us walk or take the bus to keep as many parking spaces open as possible for potential customers.

"Sounds like him," interjected Eamon. "You don't have a car of your own, Samuel?"

"Still saving in my piggy bank. Does anyone live nearby?" Faces looked down in reply.

"I'll drive you, Samuel," called a voice from the front entrance.

Sam looked down a row of desks and saw the speaker. "Come for a visit Barnaby?" Sam took long strides to reach the pastor. "Well, your timing is good. Providence at work."

"Providence, yes. I came to close my account when I heard you were taking over."

"Gee, thanks." Sam said, passing him by. "Providence is going to make you wait until tomorrow, let's get a move on!"

The Reverend hurried back to the street. Sam threw himself into Barnaby's car, an older Buick, the moment the white-haired preacher unlocked the passenger door. Barnaby insisted on driving, and frowned at the way his car rocked from Sam's hurried embarking. Staring at Eamon and Gayle, still on the curb, Barnaby said, "Are those two coming along as well?"

"How 'bout it Eamon?" Sam yelled out the window.

The angel stood his ground and shook his head. He seemed taken aback when Gayle ghosted herself into the back seat. Barnaby shuddered at the entrance.

"I intended to bring you back to the administration building," Eamon said to Gayle. "We could Return again if an agent deemed further assistance necessary."

Gayle settled into the middle of the back seat. "There's a chance that they'll skip the auditorium and drive right on to Mrs. Rockwell's house. I think I'd better come along to spot them if they pass us."

"Very well," Eamon said with a sigh. He saw the concern on Sam's face as the car began to pull onto the road. "I have your father watching over your mother," he said, trying to alleviate his worry. "I'm sure she'll be fine."

Sam nodded. He didn't like leaving his mother with only his father's protection. Still, she was safe enough for now, and Amelia needed him.

No one spoke for some time as Barnaby piloted the vehicle south toward the city of Portland. "Tell me something, Rockwell," Gayle said, the first to break the silence. "Do you have those atomic plans now that your father's gone?"

"There are no plans," Sam said, sounding more annoyed than he intended. "My father made it up and I have no idea why."

"I never took," Barnaby paused as he made a turn, "your father to be a bearer of false witness."

"Neither did I," Sam muttered. The discussion was irritating him. Amelia's life was now in danger, and all for a diagram or file that didn't even exist. For the first time in his life, Sam felt something bordering on disdain for his father. Why on earth or in heaven did he make up that bit about atomic secrets? Just for another couple of days of complaining about life in general? It didn't make any sense. Sam shook the thought aside, growing more agitated.

"There's a two-hour window beginning at noon when you'll be able to corner Dimitry," Gayle said, changing the subject. "He might be competing when we arrive, so your best bet is to try and catch him and Leonard after he's done. It'll be loads of help if Dimitry is already winded."

"Hopefully Miss Martin will still be with them, safe and sound," offered Barnaby.

Sam butted his head against the window, longing for the earlier quiet time. He wanted to think, and the Reverend's attempts at cheerful optimism weren't helping.

"Like I said, there's a chance that the two of them bypass Portland with Amelia," Gayle said. "It would mean ditching Dimitry's cover, but if they feel like it's what's needed to get those plans—"

"There aren't any plans," Sam said shortly. He opened his mouth to apologize, but Gayle cut him off.

"Come on, Rockwell," she said, flavoring her voice with a Siren's allure. "You both just said Frank wasn't a liar. What's the sense of him coming back otherwise? You can let me know who has the plans, it's not like I can do anything with them."

"Why do you care?" Sam said. Something felt off. Gayle's response wasn't what he expected. He was sure his outburst would have hurt her feelings. Returns were generally a touchy bunch. Recent death tended to have that effect.

Gayle blew out her breath in the direction of her bangs. It seemed strange to Sam that ghosts still could make those sorts of mannerisms, in spite of no longer needing to breath. Perhaps the effect was for the comfort of the living. "I suppose," she said, "I just want to go wherever I'm heading knowin' that I didn't die for some stupid misunderstanding. If the plans exist, and I help restore them, then maybe my part on earth was for something after all."

Sam remained quiet. He felt empathy for the Return. She'd probably had a difficult life. Everyone lives their life knowing they're going to die. What must it be like to reach the end and know that, without a miracle, the life you led was wasted or without meaning? "I wish I could help," he said, "but there aren't any plans. My father was a financial, not nuclear, adviser."

"Well," said Gayle, "I can tell you for certain that Dimitry and Leonard believe otherwise. It's all they could talk about in—" she paused, "in those last few moments."

"I'm sorry," Sam managed. He felt odd apologizing to his father's killer, but couldn't think of anything else to say.

Barnaby nodded his head in agreement. "You see, Samuel," he said, taking the tone of a lecturer, "death in all its forms is a terrible abomination. You'd do well to leave this world's casual and flippant acceptance of it."

Sam ground his teeth. The world, life, and death were all much too large for him at the moment. Light from the morning sun temporarily transformed the glass of Sam's passenger door window. It grew opaque and reflective. Sam observed the still healing cuts and bruises on his face. They were nearly gone, red gashes having given way to a soft, embossed pink. It occurred to Sam that another scrap may be in order. Shooting among a crowd, or near Amelia wasn't the best course of action.

Muscles tensed as Sam played back his fight at the tavern on the night he'd first run into the two goons. How many lives like Gayle's and his Father's had they ruined? Sam vowed not to let him and Amelia be added to their list.

The Reverend spoke up, again. "May I ask you some questions young lady?" Barnaby glanced at Gayle in the rear-view mirror.

She shifted in her seat. "What about? The afterlife? Some kind of professional curiosity?"

Keeping his eyes fixed on the road ahead, Barnaby calmly replied, "About you, and the state of your soul."

"A little late for that, wouldn't you say?"

"Ordinarily I would say, yes. And as it is appointed unto men once to die, but after this the judgment. Hebrews the ninth chapter, verse twenty-seven."

Gayle guffawed from the back seat. "But here I am."

"Here you are," Barnaby echoed. "And since you're here, I wish to redeem the time by quoting the verse which follows: So Christ was once offered to bear the sins of many; and unto them that look for him shall he appear the second time without sin unto salvation."

Sam stirred slightly in his seat. "Reverend Barnaby is trying to make sure you take the elevator up."

A cloud darkened Gayle's countenance. "I'm helping make things right, ain't I?"

"Help is a wonderful thing." Barnaby's words were soothing and carried an authority that comes from long living, like a grandparent commiserating the pains of youth. "However, it's not help, but reconciliation that you need. I think that should be our purpose."

Satisfied that his point was made and heard, Barnaby took to whistling. The tunes slowed and he licked his lips. "I must admit that I was taken up in this emergency without fully considering the matter. Why don't we simply pull over and call upon the police for help?"

"Tried that," Sam fidgeted in his seat, desperate to move faster. "They won't listen."

"If the local police won't help," Barnaby said, "call the Portland police."

Gayle laughed, not quite mocking. "They won't believe you," she said. "And if they did, Dimitry and Leonard would kill the girl."

The Portland Auditorium loomed a block ahead through the front windshield. Barnaby drove as fast as his trembling hands allowed, but it seemed molasses-like to Sam.

"We've almost arrived," Barnaby stated.

Sam drummed his hands against the dashboard. "Pull up next to the main entrance to let us out."

From the back seat, Gayle sized up Sam and Barnaby, glancing at the approaching building. She pursed her lips and suddenly stood straight up. No longer anchored to the vehicle, the car passed through her ghostly form, leaving her standing in the street. A trailing car blared its horn and swerved to avoid the apparition.

Checking his rearview from the noise, Barnaby gasped at the empty seat. He slammed on his breaks, causing the car to lurch forward. A new series of horns sounded behind him. "Samuel! Gayle jumped out and is running straight through whatever lies before her."

"What?" Sam leaned out the window and watched as Gayle ran through every obstacle on her way toward the Auditorium. His stomach sank as he called after her, "Hey!"

Gayle turned as she moved, running through a sandwich

board for a nearby deli. "Death to world capitalism!" she shouted at Sam and then disappeared through the Auditorium's main entryway.

Barnaby's transparently blue eyes stared at Sam through furrowed bushy eyebrows. "I don't think she's on our side, Samuel."

"She seems intent on taking an elevator down." Sam pulled himself tall and pointed to the Auditorium. "Step on it and get me to those stairs!"

The car screeched to a halt in front of the entrance. Sam swung open the passenger door and nearly tumbled onto the curb. "Please Lord, keep Amelia safe."

"You have just made the soundest decision available to you." Barnaby reached over to close the door behind Sam. He called after him, "He teacheth my hands to war so that a bow of steel is broken by mine arms."

Sam nodded as he ran to the Auditorium's entrance, not quite sure what Barnaby meant. If it was a prayer that Sam would break Dimitry's arm when he found him, he'd take it. Leaping steps two at a time, he opened the auditoriums main doors, passing a ticket attendant as he rushed inside. The attendant, caught up in reading, dropped his book as Sam sped past, a furious wind.

"Hey," shouted the attendant, "we're sold out."

Sam continued toward the main auditorium without so much as a backward glance. A police officer poked his head around the corner. "Some guy's glomming the price of admission," the attendant said, jabbing his thumb after Sam's trail. The officer took a stutter-step and began to jog.

Gayle must have made her way in more subtly than he had.

Too late to change that now. Sam reached his arms out and disappeared through a pair of double doors. The murmur of the auditorium's buzzing crowd filled his ears. A mixture of stale sweat and cigarette smoke hung pungent in the air. All the lighting was fixed on a ring at the center of the auditorium's arena.

Sam's eyes adjusted to the darkness and looked down to the ring. Inside, two men, shirtless and wearing trunks, circled one another, tentatively raising hands and locking up in a test of strength. Neither man was anywhere near large enough to be Dimitry. Gayle was right about one thing, professional wrestling was the perfect cover for the big Soviet.

Remembering the police officer, Sam hurried his way down the stairs and past rows of seats. He turned back and saw light appear from the opening door. The officer would be inside soon. Sam couldn't afford to be slowed down or found out, even if the man was only doing his job.

A roar shot up from the crowd as one of the men in the ring flipped the other over his back, sending him crashing down hard onto the canvas floor. The crowd continued to roar, standing in unison as the grappler took the opportunity afforded to him by the back-body drop. He flung himself on top of the other wrestler and covered him.

Sam saw an opportunity of his own, and forced his way among a row of spectators, joining in the revelry as the referee counted to three in the ring. More cheers cascaded down to the victor, and Sam watched from the corner of his eye as the officer walked past him and down the stairs.

The ring announcer gave the official decision, win by pinfall, the time of the match, and went on to inform the crowd that there would be a twenty-minute intermission as the television broadcast went backstage for another dressing room interview.

Fans began to make their way to the various concessions. Sam watched as the winner of the match exited the ring and disappeared behind a black curtain, the loser shortly following. Behind that curtain was where he'd find Dimitry. Hopefully Amelia, too.

Watching the flow of bodies, Sam allowed himself to be swept up in its current. Casually, he made his way around the auditorium, inching closer to the wrestler's backstage area. It would be a risk to try and enter by jumping across the railing, in full view of the public, then dashing behind the scenes. The risk seemed faster than the alternative. There weren't any security officials standing by the curtain, and he was sure that wouldn't be the case if he tried to get backstage through a loading dock.

Either way, Sam didn't have the luxury of anything but the direct route. Amelia's very life was in danger. Gayle said Dimitry and Leonard were willing to kill her. Sam felt that much of her story was true, and time was nearly out.

There was no sign of the police officer, perhaps he was looking for Sam nearer the concession stands. Or maybe he gave up on the hunt altogether.

Following the crowd, he came to the point where two streams of flowing human traffic met at an exit. He deftly cut across an aisle to the seats on the other side, swimming through the surging column of spectators as they sought restrooms or popcorn. Walking like he stood on a window ledge, Sam edged past the fans that remained in their seats. They pulled their knees back or stood as he passed them by. "Pardon me. Excuse me, sir. Apologies, ma'am."

The black curtained entrance leading backstage, to Amelia, was now directly below Sam. He hoped there would be enough people returning to their seats to mask his approach to the railing. He wanted cover right up to the moment he hopped over and bound backstage. Instead, Sam was greeted with a throng of people still making their way up to the exits. He took a deep breath, as if to dive beneath the human waves, and began cutting a path downward.

Moving against the grain of the crowd was slow going, but Sam was making gradual progress. The black curtain ebbed closer. Another fifteen rows or so and he'd be there.

Almost there, Amelia. Hold on.

A shout came from somewhere behind Sam. He knew it was for him. It was distant, though. If he pretended not to notice, maybe the policeman would let it go. A murmur rippled through the crowd and Sam knew he was being chased. He stole a glance and saw the officer trying vainly to make his way down.

"You down there!" the officer shouted, his voice slightly muted by the humming crowd. "Stop right now!"

Just great. Sam put his head down and heaved his broad shoulders into what human resistance remained before him. Shouts of surprise and annoyance called out as he plowed his way to the guardrail. He peered up at the officer again. The crowd was giving way to him and he made rapid gains. "I said stop!"

Grabbing the metal railing, Sam hurled himself over, landing in a crouch and scurrying behind the curtain. The black drapery led to a dank hall that smelled faintly of urine. Whatever glamor the other side of entryway provided the television cameras, the backstage area had none. A few boxes and papers were strewn haphazardly on the floor. Folding chairs were stationed carelessly along the walls.

There was no sign of Dimitry, or any other wrestler for that matter. Just a couple of backstage hands who were either completely oblivious, or doing their best to ignore Sam until security arrived. He didn't wait for that to happen.

Gayle seemed to have disappeared. Sam hoped she was recalled. He moved swiftly down the long corridor hallway, pausing at each doorway long enough to edge himself and peer inside. The hall seemed to go on forever. Sam thought it must run parallel along the entire building.

Most of the rooms were open, many without even a door. Sam came to an exception, a wooden door with chipped white paint revealing an earlier shade of green beneath. He turned the handle and heard a clatter and skid on the other side, like furniture scraping across a cement floor.

Inside, the room was dark. Sam fumbled for a light switch. He found one, and pressed the button. A warm glow ushered from what seemed to be stage lights above. On the floor, tipped on its side, was a wooden chair. Coils of rope loosely wrapped around the legs and back of the chair. Sam felt the seat for warmth. Stone cold.

Amelia had to have been here, and by the state of the room Sam sensed her captors were in a rush to clear her out. Still, she'd been gone long enough for whatever body heat the chair held to dissipate. Could be minutes or hours, he thought. A real detective probably would know.

Sam reached inside his jacket for his pistol. Where was his pistol? Sam rolled his eyes and muttered a clumsy oath against himself. He'd left the gun on his desk, one-hundred and fifty miles away. With no pistol, he stole quietly out of the room, wary that Leonard or Dimitry might know already of his arrival. Why else leave in such a hurry?

Further up the hall, he spotted Gayle. She hadn't disappeared after all. She gasped at the sight of him and turned to run into another door way. Before she could pass through or enter, she disappeared. "Returned for good," Sam said to himself.

Sam was sure she tipped Leonard and Dimitry off. He was angry at himself for not realizing her duplicity sooner, back when she kept asking about the atomic secrets. Gayle died for Frank's lie, all right, but as a willing believer in it. She sacrificed herself to become a sort of double agent in death.

"We all die, right?" Sam muttered to himself. He ran down the hall to where she last stood. Gayle couldn't have done too much damage. She would have only had five, maybe ten minutes to warn the communists. Sam decided he would make sure they weren't still in the building and then rejoin Barnaby to chase them to their final destination—his parent's home.

"Stop right now! I'm not warning you again, pal!"

The police officer's voice boomed from back by the curtain. He must have gotten held up in the crowd and temporarily lost Sam. He had him now, though. The officer set out on a reluctant run and Sam could hear his wheezes echoing down the corridor.

Sam was out of the starting blocks in a full sprint, feeling wind on his face as it whipped in his ears. He could outrun the officer, but he needed to be sure Amelia wasn't in the building. He slowed slightly at each doorway he came to. Nothing.

He turned a corner, the officer still a good deal behind him.

Sam was fairly certain the man had stopped for air. Another man wearing a button-down shirt waved his hands at Sam, demanding silence. A glowing red sign above the man read, "ON AIR."

Sam slowed to a jog, much to the man's silently fuming consternation. But as he reached the door, he skidded himself to a halt. He knew the voice coming from the other side.

CHAPTER THIRTEEN

The only instructions Eamon gave Frank were to watch Alice and call for help if there was trouble. At the time, Frank hadn't thought about who or how he might call. Now that he stood Returned in his front lawn, he wished he had.

Frank squeezed his thumb against the rest of his hand. The entire Return process would run a lot smoother if someone would put him in charge.

Surveying the yard, he let out a cluck with his tongue. The emerald lawn had grown too rough, with stray blades of grass out-pacing the pack, calling to be cut back down. He sighed. At least someone remembered to water.

Suppressing the urge to soliloquize on the value of a well

maintained lawn, Frank pushed onward with his mind fixed on Alice. This must be his last chance to see her. Captain Buford was right about not being sent back again. If it weren't for whatever trouble those friends of Gayle were up to, he knew he would not see his wife until she joined him... he buried the thought.

The twinkle of sunlight on chrome caught his eye, and Frank detoured onto his driveway. He most wanted to see Alice, but he also didn't mind the chance to see his baby once more. Arriving at the car, he swallowed hard upon seeing a sign in the rear window of the Cadillac.

"For Sale," Frank read out loud. The sign was large, with bold red letters that called eagerly for admirers. Frank clutched his chest in a mock cardiac arrest. Had he not already been deceased, the sight of seeing his gleaming black beauty ready to be auctioned off to the highest bidder, like a heifer at the farmer's market, would have done him in.

Losing control, he thrust a finger upward. "Alice," he called, quickening his pace toward the door. A tornado of emotion spun inside Frank, spurring him to a confrontation. He was ready to storm through the door like Normandy, but remembered himself. He took a deep breath, then another. He was sure no air was circulating inside his ghostly lungs, but the exercise calmed him all the same.

"Last chance, Rockwell," he said to himself. He looked down at a venerable welcome mat. "Remember why you came back in the first place."

Like a breeze finding an open window, Frank went through the front door. He heard Alice singing to herself somewhere upstairs. He rocked his head from side to side. "Clearly I've been missed."

His wife sang on, unaware of her husband's third Return. "Alice!" he called, thankful to have left his frustrations over the Cadillac in the driveway. He needed to get things going on the right foot. "Alice, they sent me back again."

The singing stopped. Frank listened, but couldn't make out a reply. He began to fear that the next noise would be his wife fainting. He strained his ears, imagining that he heard several thuds before her footsteps sounded down the first set of stairs.

"Frank? Is that you?" Alice descended the remaining stairs and saw her husband standing near the coat rack. She gave a fractional frown. "'til death do we part, my foot."

Frank's blood boiled in an instant. "Oh, ho! See how the widow Rockwell—" He abruptly silenced himself.

Alice expected the outburst, she'd all but asked for it. She had been a dutiful wife, patiently enduring her husbands tantrums in life. That time was past. He was dead and she shouldn't have to deal with them from beyond the grave.

With squinted eyes, she examined her husband. Frank never cut his eruptions short. She readied herself for battle, unsure of where Frank was going and expecting a verbal trap. "That's all you have to say? That's a first, Frank."

Frank measured his voice like a tailor sizing a suit. He wanted to be careful to keep his words from cutting too deeply. This opportunity wouldn't last long. He couldn't waste time fighting. "Well, never mind that, dear. I'm glad to see you again all the same." A suspiciously raised eyebrow was his only reply. Frank patted his trousers absentmindedly. There was so little time. He could be recalled at any moment and that would be that. He groped for the keys that used to haunt his pockets, a nervous habit.

The keys! He knew at once how to relieve Alice of her skepticism.

"I see that you put my baby... er... the Cadillac up for sale."

Alice folded her arms and pushed her hips out to one side. So this was to be Frank's Waterloo. The car. Of course.

She took in a breath, ready to fend off the cantankerous speech that was sure to follow. She waited. A fiery diatribe should have already begun.

Frank instead stood quietly, as if contemplating what move to next make. "I suppose that makes sense," he said at last.

Alice dropped her hands to her sides. Frank removed his spectral hat and put it on the coat rack. "It was my car, and I won't be needing it. You might as well sell it while the value is high and get something better suited to your needs."

Mrs. Rockwell could not believe what she was hearing. She circled her husband, eying him up and down. The ghost in the front room certainly looked like Frank.

"I'm proud of you, Alice," Frank said, smiling at his wife as she walked around him. "The dealerships will never pay you what you can get through a little hard work of your own."

"Frank?" Alice said, stopping to look him face to face. There was no mistaking those eyes, the same ones Sam had been born with. "Frank Rockwell?"

"Now don't tease me, Ally." He bowed his head low and looked to her, earnestly, through upturned eyes.

She had not been called 'Ally' since their first years of marriage. "Why are you back? What's happened? Is something wrong?"

Frank looked tenderly at his wife. A deep love of many years caught up with him. He felt like a fool for his distracted life, now ended. He was like a man who missed his youthful vitality only when his knees and back refused to move him from his chair. He realized his loss only when it was gone. So very much had been lost.

"Alice, I love you."

Her hands shot for her heart, groping for this most unexpected missile from Cupid's bow. She was taken aback, and thought for a moment that Frank might take her reaction for mocking and rupture into a shouting monologue. Instead, he dropped to his knee.

"I'm sorry, Ally."

There was no doubt about it. The voice Sam heard through the door was Dimitry's, the big Russian who nearly pulverized his face two weeks ago. At least, it sounded like him.

Sam turned the handle, opening the door slightly ajar. The production assistant standing outside the door grabbed Sam's sleeve, trying to keep the door from opening any further. "Are you nuts?!" the assistant whispered. "Jules is live on television right now, you can't go in there!"

But the opening of the door, slight as it was, left no room for doubt. Dimitry was on the other side, talking about his love for America of all things. Sam shook the production assistant's grip and threw open the door, finding Dimitry and the interviewer's backs to him, with a shocked cameraman aiming his lens right at him. Sam had never been on television before. Here was a nice story to make friends in Los Angeles jealous, if he ever made it back.

Dimitry angled his head to the commotion. Sam pounced on him like a jaguar from a tree limb, causing "Crusher Koskov" to crash down onto his back. Sam knew from watching a few wrestling matches with his father that he'd just executed a perfect Lou Thesz press. Sitting on Dimitry's chest, Sam hammered at the Russian's granite jaw while the host screamed for order.

Sam's advantage was only temporary. Dimitry quickly grabbed his attacker's wrists and used Sam's momentum to half-throw, half-pull, him over his head. Sam hit the floor on his hands and knees.

"Is one of Baron's spies," Dimitry screamed, dedicated to his craft. "He wants to take me prisoner back to Soviet Union." He scrambled out the door and off camera. Sam rose and stumbled after him, brushing aside the host's attempts to detain him.

Turning his face to the viewers at home, Jules Owen raised his microphone and smiled, attempting to salvage the segment. "Our next guest is a young man who needs no introduction—"

The production assistant closed the door as Sam chased after Dimitry down the hall. Long strides quickly made up the slight distance the wrestler managed to put between himself and Sam. Leaping into the air, Sam threw both of his knees into the fleeing Russian's back, sending him skidding on the floor. Dimitry stopped with a squeak, and barely had time to put his palms in a push-up position before Sam jumped again onto his back, slamming the Russian's forehead onto the floor with an echoing thud, like a watermelon dropped in an alley.

"Where is she?!" Sam gasped, trying vainly to grab a handful of shortly cropped hair. He squeezed his hands around Dimitry's temple. It felt like he was holding a medicine ball.

"Is dead," Dimitry said, struggling to shake off Sam and the effects of the blows all at once. "My partner finishes her off when Gayle say you no have plans. Now he visit your mother. If she no have plans, she die too."

A cold draught of horror poured into Sam's stomach. It was replaced with a white-hot rage. He slammed Dimitry's head face-first onto the floor, hearing a familiar thick, wet crunch. Pulling the wrestler's head back up, Sam was poised to deliver another blow when someone pulled him off.

"I said that's enough!" It was the officer. Together with the production assistant, he hurled Sam against a corridor wall. Sam sat on the floor with one leg up, fuming, too angry to speak. Dimitry lay prone, groaning as a small pool of blood formed around his head.

The officer turned to the production assistant, panting from exertion. "Find Officer Davis and get him down here." The other man took off sprinting. Returning his attention to Sam, the officer's hand hovered over his holster. "Sit. Right. There."

Dimitry struggled to his knees and put a hand to his nose. Drawing it back, he stared at his blood-soaked palm. He put his hands on his tree-trunks of quadriceps, smearing them red. Slowly, he rose to his full, imposing height, like a plume of sulfuric smoke ascending from the depths of hell. He took a heavy step toward Sam, all menace and wrath. Blood was rushing down his face, splattering on his chest like drops of red rain.

"Hold on, Koskov," said the officer, seeing the murderous

rage in the big man's eyes. He signaled for the wrestler to halt. "I know this fink jumped you and banged you up, but we have to—"

A pair of massive hands wrapped around the officer's head and face, muffling whatever final words he uttered. His eyes transfixed on Sam, Dimitry gave a violent twist to the policeman's head, causing the neck to snap and crunch like a stalk of celery. Sam sprang to his feet as the officer's lifeless body dropped hard.

Uttering a guttural scream, Dimitry lunged at Sam, throwing the full force of his bulk into the corridor wall as Sam nimbly sidestepped the attack.

"I kill you," screamed Dimitry, wiping still more blood onto his forearm and advancing again. His eyes were beady and dark with unbridled anger.

Moving backward, Sam began to pepper the wrestler's face with a myriad of jabs, snapping his head back and causing a crimson mask to spread across his face and dye his blond flattop. Sam's knuckles were coated in red gore, but Dimitry was oblivious to the blows.

Sam planted his feet and connected hard with a left to the Russian's ribs. If he could stun the mountain, he might have time to retrieve the dead officer's firearm. He followed with a right uppercut, but Dimitry swatted the punch aside with one hand. He pushed Sam hard in the middle of his chest, nearly taking the wind out of him. Sam wavered, and almost kept his balance but for the body of the policeman clipping his heel and causing him to fall, landing hard on his tail bone.

With swiftness altogether unexpected, Dimitry leapt onto Sam. The force of his weight crashing on top of him sent out an involuntary grunt. Sam held Dimitry's wrists tightly in each hand, unable to wrap his fingers fully around their staggering circumference. The Russian flexed his forearms and nearly broke Sam's grip.

"You will die now," Dimitry said, bearing down on his prey. He forced his hands to Sam's neck. "I kill you! You die!"

Globs of blood and spittle showered down on Sam's face and clothing as he tried vainly to match the Russian's power and hold back his strangling hands. He felt them squeeze around his neck like a noose. The gasping breaths Sam had relied on for oxygen were cut out, bringing black and white spots before his eyes. His throat was too constricted for even a gurgle.

Kicking one leg free of Dimitry's bulk, Sam searched the ground frantically with heel, hoping to find something he could kick to arm's reach and use to knock Dimitry off of him. He found nothing but empty space in an empty corridor.

Sam felt his energy sapping away.

The pressure and strain on his face, nearly purple, was excruciating. His eyes were closing of their own accord. He let go of Dimitry with his right hand, hoping to use it to gouge an eye. The grip somehow tightened. Sam put everything he had into the punch, but it landed impotent on Dimitry's face. The Russian brushed the soft slap away with a roll of his neck.

Sam's eyes closed again. The pain in his head and neck seemed to fade. Darkness swallowed him, darkness and a high-pitched ringing in his ears. I'm going to be choked to death, Sam thought. A vision of Amelia, sitting among the wildflowers, appeared to him. Sam smiled, though his face couldn't show it. The high-pitched ring gave way to a sudden thump, and Sam felt a muffled jolt through his body. A shock-wave of pain returned to his face, neck and, especially, his throat. Feeling like an elephant was sitting on his chest, Sam heard heavy gasping breaths and realized they were his own.

He could breathe!

Sam's eyes fluttered open. Instead of seeing Dimitry above him, he saw Eamon holding a pistol in his hand, the butt of the weapon sticking out and covered with still more blood. "I—" Sam stopped and took a breath. He tasted copper from the back of his raw throat. "I thought ghosts couldn't interact with the physical world."

"I told you, old bean," Eamon said, "I'm an angel, not a Return. Let's get you up." He hoisted Sam on two feet and steadied him as he wavered. "There you are. You'll be all right soon enough. More police will be here soon, we'd do well to let them come across this scene without you being present. There's an exit this way."

Daylight engulfed the men as they opened the side exit and made their way toward Reverend Barnaby, who was still parked in his car, reading his Bible.

"He said Amelia was dead," Sam managed to croak out.

"She's alive. I would have seen her upstairs. I instructed my clerks to alert me immediately if anyone involved in this shenanigan arrived at the Pearly Gates."

Sam breathed a sigh of relief, his shoulders shaking from the nervous fatigue of almost losing her twice in one day. First thinking her dead, then nearly dying himself.

"But," Eamon continued, "that doesn't mean that she's out of danger. The other man, Leonard, was warned—"

"By Gayle," Sam said.

Eamon stopped. "How the deuce did you know that?"

"She couldn't keep her Communist mouth shut. I figure she let them kill her to have a better chance at getting... well, at getting the secrets my father made up." They reached the side of the car.

"Indeed," said Eamon. "You ought to be licensed with us. As for Gayle, we recalled her the moment we discovered what was really happening, but the damage had already been done."

Barnaby looked up from his devotions at the two men. He stuck his head out of the car's window. "Did she... repent?"

Eamon shook his head. "I'm afraid not. Straight down with her nose in the air and curses for all." The Reverend's face saddened. "Don't get down on yourself, old bean. I hear you did a knock-up job giving her the news. Not your fault she spurned it, now is it?"

"So Amelia," Sam said, changing the subject.

"Right," Eamon answered, snapping his finger. "You'd better get going. He has a lead on you. Heading straight for your mother's house."

Barnaby inspected the blood on Sam's hands, face, and clothing. "I take it that what happened within the auditorium was not a civil discord?"

"Two beatings and a murder," Sam said, rubbing his throat.

"I may further assume the murderer was not you?"

"No," Sam said, a little hurt, "the Russian."

Barnaby shook his head. "The hero of Cascade Wrestling commits a murder, and you, the man who fought him, are leaving the scene of the crime so he can give his version of events, leave the city, and have the police search you out?"

"I hadn't thought of that," Eamon said. "Someone has to stay and let the police know what's happening."

Sam danced from one foot to the next. "I've gotta get a move on and save Amelia and my Mother."

Letting out a sigh, Eamon said, "I'm afraid I can't be further involved at this level. I need to get back to my command room."

"That leaves me to stay behind and see things through," said Barnaby, stepping out from behind the wheel.

"Great," Sam said, practically running in place. "Just hand me the keys and I'll get going."

Barnaby leered in disbelief. "I'm not giving you my car. I need it. Have this angel fly you home."

"Technically," Eamon said, flashing a complacent smile, "I can only take people to a when, not a where. And even that is allowable only for licensed detectives."

"So you can take me through time, but not to Tacoma? Great."

"Just so." Eamon stuck two fingers to his lips and let loose a piercing whistle. "I did think of a contingency escape, however. I had one of our men, well, one of our angels, follow you down. He drives a taxi for his cover. The roads need more and more guardians, you see."

The same driver that nearly killed Sam and Amelia in transporting them from the airport, still thin as a nail, pulled into the lot. With a grin, he got out and opened the back door to his cab.

Sam looked to Eamon, curling his lip. "Well, at least I know he'll drive fast."

"What's gotten into you, Frank," Alice said for the fifth or sixth time since her husband had walked back into her life. He had been following her around the house like a lovesick puppy.

"I told you Ally, I love you."

"I heard you, but I assumed you loved me before you died, and you never acted then like you are now."

Frank paused and for a moment, Alice thought he was going to give up on his charade and let loose a scathing defense of himself. "I know," he said with reluctance. "And I'm sorry. Do you remember the night I died?"

"Vividly."

"Right. Well, you asked me on that night why I was sent back."

"And you said you didn't know why," Alice said, gathering up some papers she needed for a telephone meeting with Collette Peterson. She would be calling any moment. The Ladies Missionary Society was left a sizable gift upon Frank's death. Alice and Collette were to decide who needed it most.

"The truth of it was I knew exactly why. I just, just didn't know how to say it."

"You mean those atomic secrets that had everyone so riled up?"

Frank splayed his palms. "Why does everyone keep bringing that up? Fine. I admit that there wasn't any danger of atomic secrets falling into anyone's hands. I only mentioned them to get back."

"For pot roast?" said Alice, but playfully.

"No, dear," Frank was so earnest that Alice felt the urge to press his nose like a button. She would sometimes do that when they were younger. Frank began anew. "I came back so I could—"

Someone knocked on the door. Frank stiffened, remembering the reason Eamon sent him back. "Were you expecting company?"

"No," said Alice, walking to the door.

"Let me check it out." Frank walked into the sofa. He stood in the middle of it and leaned his head out the window to peer at whoever was standing at the front door. He quickly ducked his head back inside.

"What in the blazes is Dale Turner doing one our front porch with a bouquet of flowers?"

"Oh, him. He's been after me shamelessly since you died. Where are you going?"

Frank marched through the front window and into the yard.

"Turner," Alice could hear Frank yell from outside. "What's the idea coming after my wife?" She leaned against the door to better hear, a smile coming to her lips like Christmas morning. Frank was fighting for her. It had been a long time.

"The good book says 'til death do you part," Turner replied, his voice muffled by the door. "You had your time with her. Why not give someone else a chance?"

Alice ducked her head and giggled. Frank loathed when Scripture was quoted at him, though she doubted that Turner or Frank could point out any such specific passage.

"Now you listen to me," Frank said. Alice imagined his finger pointed just inches away from Turner's face. "Alice is my girl. I don't care if I'm dead or not. As long as I'm around, nobody is going to tell her what a loving, beautiful, decent, kind, wonderful, sweet, and magnificent woman she is but me." Alice crossed her hands and smiled. Words like these used to flow freely in her husband's love letters, only to be replaced by formulaic poems on greeting cards with his signature at the bottom.

"I told her all that last week," Turner challenged. "And when you disappear, I'll tell her again."

The phone rang. Alice ignored it, listening eagerly for Frank's response.

"The hell you say. Listen to me once and for all Turner. If you so much as put one foot on our front lawn ever again, I'll haunt you for the rest of your miserable life. I've been dead for a while and I'm still here, so you know I can do it." Alice gasped, and then laughed from behind the door.

"All right, Frank," Turner said. His voice sounded shaky. He was rattled. "I'm going, I'm going."

Frank walked back inside the house, dusting off his hands as he did so. He paused and leaned his head back outside. "I'd have kicked you as you went, but you wouldn't have felt it."

Alice clapped her hands, "That was impressive, Frank. I don't think he'll be back again."

"He'd better not be."

She moved toward him, forgetting in the moment her inability to touch him, feel him again. The phone rang again, stopping her short. "That's Collette," she said, walking to the television and twisting the knob on. "Why don't you watch your show while I talk to her? It's Saturday, after all."

"Thank you, dear." Frank took a seat on the couch instead of his usual chair. "I'll await your return like the first blooms of spring." Alice left for the upstairs telephone.

Frank rubbed his hands and waited for the television to warm up. Soon, the screen's soft glow emanated from its mahogany wood cabinet. A tall, but portly man in a black suit came on screen, holding a microphone while looking directly into the camera.

"How do you do, ladies and gentlemen," the man said, "Jules Owen here in the dressing room and once again, it's time for Dressing Room Interviews." Behind the man was a closed white door, with two rows of coat pegs on either side. A silk jacket hung on a peg, shimmering under the television lights.

Good, thought Frank. He tuned in just in time.

"Our first guest this afternoon," the host said, smiling, "one of the biggest, most powerful, and I might say outstandingly conditioned athlete of our time. Of course I'm speaking of big Crusher Koskov."

"Hello, Jules," said the massive Russian, appearing from off screen and gingerly shaking hands. He was shirtless, and even through the hazy black and white screen, Frank could see his muscles rippling with every subtle movement.

Frank clapped his hands and let out a holler. "Crusher Koskov. Soviet defector and lover of the American way of life. My sort of hero." He bit his lip, worried that his outburst might have carried up the stairs and bothered Alice.

Back on screen, Koskov and the host continued their interview. "Now, Crusher," the host said, "you know a lot of people ask me, they say, 'Gee this fella has got the biggest neck I ever saw he's in the best condition I ever saw for a big man,' how 'bout tellin' us some of the secrets of how you do train?"

The camera zoomed on Crusher. "Is true, but is long story—"

"Well, we can't have all of it but we should have time for some tips," the host interrupted, smiling into the camera.

"I have gymnasium picked out in every wonderful U.S.A. city I visit. My neck is twenty-two inches." The big Russian flexed his neck and shoulder for the camera. "This is from training at least two hour, every day."

"That's the sort of discipline needed to keep up your physique? I know some of the male wrestling fans watching at home, and certainly the many female fans, would like to know how you manage to keep your waist so trim as well."

"Ha-ha," laughed Koskov, he clapped his interviewer's shoulder and looked at the camera. "Is one of my secrets. But, I say this. You want achieve success? You must dedicate and work hard, like American way. When I work for Soviet government, no hard work anywhere. No sacrifice. This is why when I tour United States; I defect to live in greatest country on earth."

Frank dashed his fist emphatically. "That's right."

The television host on screen seemed to share Frank's enthusiasm for Koskov. With a smile nearly as wide as his chest, he said, "What can you tell us about your upcoming heavyweight championship match with Baron Von Fritz for the Cascade Wrestling heavyweight championship?"

Frank leaned forward to soak up every word. He hated the Nazi-sympathizing Baron. The door behind Koskov began to move. Frank watched as it abruptly swung open. A young man wearing a suit flew into the room and tackled Koskov, knocking him over. The pair crashed to the ground off camera while Jules Owen looked on in stunned disbelief.

"Alice, you've got to see this," Frank said, jumping to his feet. He instantly regretted this outburst as well. To his surprise, Alice stood already in the living room, holding a book of some sort. Probably a journal for the Ladies Missionary Society.

"I'm sorry, Ally. I got caught up in this fight. Must be one of the Baron's men trying to take Koskov out before the title match."

Alice walked in front of the television screen. Jules Owen's was shouting for help while simultaneously trying to assure the viewers that the interview would continue momentarily.

For a moment, Frank leaned sideway to try to see around Alice. He looked up at her hesitant eyes, smiled, and sat back down on the sofa. Alice turned off the television set, and Frank didn't complain.

"Missionary business all taken care of?"

"No," said Alice, joining him on the sofa. "But I thought there might be better ways to spend the time. While you're still here, that is. I told Collette I'd call her another day." She opened the book resting on her lap, its aged leather creaking in protest.

"What's that?"

"Our wedding album and honeymoon pictures. I know you don't like looking at those older photos, but I thought—"

"I can think of nothing I'd like to do more."

"Really?"

"Almost nothing. But I'm dead, you know."

CHAPTER FOURTEEN

The flood of light seared Amelia's eyes with pain. She raised her tightly bound hands to bring some shade and relief. She was tired of being tied up. She had hoped that at some point during the excruciating drive she would have been able to free herself, but no such opportunity presented itself.

Apparently Leonard thought the same, and as Amelia's eyes adjusted she saw his pistol pointed directly at her. He was prepared for any attempt she might make at fighting back.

"Get out while no one's looking," he demanded, one hand holding the trunk door open. He waved his gun with the other hand, adding gravity to his words.

Amelia pushed herself up on an elbow, then sat upright, nearly hitting her head on the trunk lid. Her body ached everywhere. Jolts of numb pain spread like influenza as arms and legs, cramped from three bumpy hours in a steel coffin, came stinging back to life with pins and needles.

Sensing no danger, Leonard holstered his gun and roughly grabbed the thin ropes around Amelia's wrists. She gave a quiet yelp of pain, in spite of herself. Now glaring, he yanked her out of the trunk, keeping the lid open to screen them from any wandering eyes. A metallic flick sounded, and Leonard set his knife to work cutting the cords from her arms.

Amelia looked at the familiar surroundings, rubbing her wrists, pink and raw. She was in Tacoma again, a few houses up the street from the home of Frank and Alice Rockwell.

"Fix your hair and straighten your dress," Leonard said, placing the knife back in his pocket. "I don't want you looking like a ten-cent call girl."

"Yes, I imagine you would know how one looked." Amelia didn't care that Leonard was armed. She would let him know who he was. She started to walk around to the side of the car, but Leonard grabbed her arm and squeezed for all he was worth.

"I need to use the mirror," she said, gritting her teeth through the pain.

"Do your best without it," Leonard said, palpable rancor in his voice. He watched her appraisingly as she fluffed her hair and shimmied her dress. She could see him leer at her legs with an obvious lechery. "You know," he said, "when this is all said and done, I might show you a thing or two even a ten-cent call girl don't know nothing about."

"You're disgusting. Sam will break your nose again before you ever have the chance."

"I have the chance right now," Leonard said, advancing on her.

She took a step back, colliding with the rear bumper and nearly falling back into the trunk. Leonard gave a sick, fractional smile and stopped short. "This is how it's going to be," Leonard said, patting his pistol through his jacket. "You and I are going to walk up to Rockwell's house. You knock on the door, and make so you go inside. I'll be right behind you. If you try and warn her, or call for some sort of help, I'll kill you. Then I'll shoot her. Then I'll find the plans over both of your dead bodies. Play nice and I'll let both of you live, on my honor."

"There aren't any secret plans."

"Get moving."

Amelia moved along the sidewalk, her captor close beside her. The way Leonard sauntered next to her, as if he were taking his girl for an afternoon stroll, gave her the sensation of nausea. They opened the gate and headed toward the Rockwell's front door. Leonard moved to skulk behind a lavender bush. He pressed against the house; neatly out of sight should anyone look through door or windows.

Pulling his gun and pointing it down, he hid the weapon behind the green and purple sprigs. Amelia watched him and crinkled her nose. He looked like a rat in hiding. She knocked three times on the front door. "What if no one is home?" she asked. That was her wish, to avoid having to bring trouble to Alice, who had been so kind to her. Though with the Cadillac still sitting in the drive way, unsold, her hopes weren't high.

"Then we wait," Leonard snarled.

They didn't have to wait long. Alice opened the door, tentatively at first, but then widely and with a jovial grin. "Amelia," she said, holding her arms out, inviting an embrace. "What are you doing here?"

Swept up in a hug, Amelia didn't answer. She stood on the front steps picking at her fingers. Alice sensed the other woman's nervousness and held her at arm's length. "Amelia what's the wrong, what's the matter?" Alice said, beginning to pull the young lady into the house. "Frank, you'll never guess who was at the door this time."

"It better not be Turner again," a voice called from inside.

"He's Returned again?" Amelia asked. With Leonard still hiding just outside, she had a good idea why. Maybe she could swing the door closed behind her and lock him out long enough to do... something. The chance, if there ever was one, faded quickly.

"My lucky day," Leonard said, appearing on the porch with his gun drawn. Alice froze and then looked to Amelia, understanding.

"I'm sorry," Amelia said as tears welled in her eyes.

"Let's the three of us have a nice little chat," Leonard said, closing the door behind him.

Frank stood with balled fists, outraged by the audacity of the thin weasely man pointing a gun at his wife and Amelia. "What's all this about?" he said.

"No more games," sneered Leonard. He pointed the gun at Amelia and then Alice, gesturing towards two spots on the opposite wall. "I want you there and you there, where I can keep an eye on all three of ya." The two women reluctantly moved against the far wall, Alice looking back to Frank.

"I want to stand by my wife," Frank said, staring daggers into the thin man. There was something familiar about his face, but he couldn't recall having ever seen the man before.

"So move," Leonard said, again waving his gun.

"What do you want with us," Frank asked, still trying to place that face.

"He wants," Amelia said, "those, um, atomic secrets you mentioned when you came back."

Alice rolled her eyes and put her hands on her hips, staring incredulously at her husband. How he managed to be more trouble dead than he was alive was beyond her. Frank stood tall and pushed his chest out. "Oh, ho! Is that what you're after? Well you can't have them."

Amelia and Alice whirled on Frank, causing Leonard to track them both with his pistol. "What?" they yelled in unison.

"I'm sorry," Frank said, "But I can't give up those secrets."

"Honestly, Frank," Alice said, "I know why you Returned, clumsy as your first two attempts were. And I'm glad for it, I love you too. But—"

"All right, shut-up." Leonard impulsively picked at a piece of lint, visible only to him, with his free hand. "Now you get me what I'm after or I'll shoot..." he swung the gun and pointed it at Alice. "Her."

Frank took a step toward the man. "Of all the cowardly, slimy, and craven men on the planet, you communists are the worst."

The bang echoed through the house, causing a ringing in everyone's ears. Frank jumped backward at the sight of the muzzle flash then spun and looked to Alice, who was pressed against the wall. Frank hurried toward her, realizing by her reaction that the bullet wasn't intended for her. He looked to where Amelia was standing. She too, was fine.

"That one was for you," the thin man said. Frank turned to look directly behind where he had been standing and studied the fresh bullet hole. Fragments of dusty plaster sprinkled onto the floor. "The next one is for your wife."

"All right," Frank said, holding his hands for the thin man to stop. "Beneath the radio cabinet."

"Frank?" Alice said, unsure of what was happening.

Amelia moved for the cabinet at Leonard's bidding. He was again speaking with waves of his gun. She lowered onto hands and knees and felt the underside of the large wooden radio. Biting her lip, she pulled out a folded piece of paper and a small, brass key.

His weapon still pointed at Amelia, Leonard motioned for her to toss the key, catching it with one hand. "Read the letter," he ordered.

Amelia cleared her throat and read. "The White House, Washington. May 10, 1949. To Mr. Frank Rockwell," she looked up to the Return, disbelief showing in her raised eyebrows. "As an American citizen, I am thankful to share this nation with men such as you. Men who show such unwavering loyalty to our great republic. You were nominated by General Farnsworth, Fort Lewis, Washington State, to become a member of the American Citizen's Defense Society."

"Frank?" Alice asked, but was hushed by Leonard.

"In keeping with his recommendation, and having been found to be above reproach, you are hereby accepted into the aforementioned program. In your hands, and the hands of other loyal American citizens, rest the future and wellbeing of the United

States. You will have received instructions for the safekeeping and nature of the attached documents. Very sincerely yours," her voice began to trail off, "Harry S. Truman."

"What does this key unlock?" Leonard asked.

Frank studied the villain carefully. "A cabinet in this house." He saw a flash of hope followed by malice in Leonard's eyes and knew that no matter what he said or did, the man would kill Alice and Amelia. Frank watched as the thin man's finger slid inside his gun's trigger guard. He had to do something soon. "But I took it out of the cabinet and hid it somewhere else."

"Where?" Leonard shouted, he pointed the weapon at Amelia, then at Alice, alternating his aim between the two women.

He was going to kill them.

Frank never felt so helpless, unable to do anything beyond giving the man the chills. He needed help. Help! He dropped to his knees, drawing the thin man's aim, and disappeared.

Reverend Barnaby walked past the Civic Auditorium's main entrance, thinking he'd have a better chance at finding an authority figure at a rear door or loading dock. From there, he would have to plead the facts and begin the process of keeping Samuel's name clear. And, hopefully, send some law enforcement help after him.

A box truck pulled out of an alley leading from the building. Barnaby waited, buttoning his austere black jacket with trembling hands. The tremors had come a few years prior, just another part of growing old, he supposed. Still, he wanted anyone who saw him to know this was important, and that meant looking his best, just like on Sundays.

Turning a corner, he followed the path the truck had come down, checking the shine on his shoes as he went. The loading ramp was a long, concrete incline with a metal rolling door securely closed. To the right of the ramp was a loading dock, also closed. Two men wearing ivy caps were leaning just below the dock door, smoking and chatting idly. Probably, the men had just finished unloading whatever was in the truck.

Barnaby saw a few concrete steps leading up to a standard door. He climbed the steep stairs, using the swinging chain-rail to help pull himself up. The men seemed not to notice. He was about to ask one of them to let him in when he saw that the door was left ajar, a scrap of splintered crating keeping it open for when the smoke break ended. Barnaby shrugged, and let himself inside.

Weaving his way through pallets of boxes and crates, the aged Reverend looked for the police. Except for the dull cheers of the crowd, the building was surprisingly quiet for a crime scene. It hadn't been that long since Eamon disappeared and Sam left for Tacoma. Maybe word hadn't spread far backstage and the police were trying to keep things quiet until they could secure the building.

After meandering aimlessly for several minutes, he found himself in a long corridor. As he neared a turn in the hall, he could hear muffled voices and the scuff of shoes ambling across the concrete floor. The noises probably would have been audible much sooner to younger ears. One of the many side effects of the condition Barnaby referred to as "A-G-E."

This was very likely it. Steadying himself with a deep inhalation, Barnaby turned the corner, expecting to see the body of the murdered police officer already beneath a sheet. What he saw instead drained the color from his face, making his faded blue eyes nearly glow against their white backdrop.

Not one, as the Reverend suspected, but two police officers lay dead—both of them with heads grotesquely torqued in unnatural positions. A pool of dark blood shone in the hall, with still more smeared along the walls, like scarlet brush strokes on a whitewashed cinder block canvas. A small group of men, some wearing satin robes and trunks, milled about looking bewildered at the carnage before them. A tall, rotund man in a dark suit—Jules Owen—seemed to be in charge of the situation, chomping a cigar and barking out orders.

"Anderson, Suzuki," the big man bellowed, pointing to a young man in a white robe and a stocky Japanese man who seemed to be cut from Mt. Fuji itself, "get ready to go as soon as this match ends. I want a thirty-minute broadway to the end the show. Wilson, you'll referee. Get going."

Barnaby's quickened pace devolved into a slight limp, a trick his right knee sometimes liked to pull. Saying a short prayer, he passed the deceased officers and thought about the sad tidings waiting for their families. He signaled to get Owen's attention.

"It was not," Barnaby said, puffing out his breath more than he would have liked, "the man you suppose. It was the big Russian you know as Koskov."

"No kidding, mac," Owen said, chewing his cigar furiously. He pointed to the production assistant Sam had eluded before disrupting the interview. The man sat against the wall, crying with his head tucked between his knees. "Most of the boys saw the last copper get it. Poor Jerry saw the whole blasted mess."

"And no one tried to stop him? Surely a pack of men in peak physical condition could have overpowered Dimitry until still more police came."

"Mister," Owen said, "You didn't see the way he tossed those cops around like rag dolls. Didn't see the rage in his eyes. There was no stopping him."

Barnaby swallowed and turned again for an exit. He had to try and catch up to Samuel and warn him of the coming storm.

The weight of the pistol in his shoulder holster added a sense of assurance to Sam. And though his cab driver was just as fast and erratic as he remembered, the extra time it had taken to retrieve the gun from his office was gnawing at him. A few minutes might be the difference between life and death for Amelia and his mother.

He had wasted even more time calling the police. They seemed ready to help until the moment he identified himself as Sam Rockwell and was hung up on. Apparently, Detective Clemons hadn't been exaggerating about how much of a laughing stock he'd become within the department.

Not willing to give up, Sam called Clemons' number directly, leaving a frantic message with whomever it was that answered his calls for him. She, at least, sounded concerned enough to perhaps follow up. Probably once she shared the message with whomever else was in the station with her, she'd ball the note up and toss it into the round file.

It would be up to him to keep his father's lie from costing anymore lives. He thought of the police officer Dimitry had murdered with the casual air of one swatting away a buzzing fly. No more, thought Sam. He would stop this today or join his brother upstairs from the effort.

The taxi cab lurched around a corner, jostling Sam in his seat as rubber tires squealed to regain traction. Sam took comfort in seeing the roads so empty. The slim driver seemed to know his thoughts and glanced at him after regaining control of the vehicle.

"Yep," he said in that backwoods drawl. It was the first words he'd spoke since telling Sam he knew the way before leaving Portland. "Lots a guardian angels busy keeping folks away 'til this all finishes up." He laughed. Like a yokel. "Some folks sure is gonna be mad at the flat tires and overheated radiators it took to keep em out a bit longer, but they'd sure as sunshine be glad if they knew what fer."

"Swell." Sam lurched forward, his head nearly crashing into the dashboard. The momentum of the screeching vehicle hurled him back in his seat upon a full stop. Sam glared at the driver. "Thanks for being so discrete."

"Sorry."

Sam looked around, expecting to see the thin man already leveling his weapon to fire on the taxi. Instead, he saw the same run-down tan house he and Amelia got out at the last time they rode on this carnival ride.

"This'll do," Sam said exiting the vehicle. "Either wait here or drive away, but quietly, huh?" The driver nodded and Sam jogged up the sidewalk, eerily quiet for a Saturday summer afternoon. He heard a distant POP that he knew to be a gunshot. He quickened his pace to an all-out sprint.

Jumping over old Mrs. Ernst's cedar fence and into his parent's yard, Sam crouched low and drew his pistol. He landed on the other side lightly, but paused and strained his ears, just in case he'd been seen. It was unlikely, he knew. Sam and his brother Elijah had spent years of childhood learning all the best sight lines for use in games of hide-n-seek and cops & robbers. He fingered the pearl handle of his weapon nervously. It seemed clear.

Sidling up to a corner window, Sam raised his eye level just above the white exterior sill. The view afforded him a field of vision that included most of the downstairs interior, except for the kitchen. He and Elijah used to spy on his mother or father through this window, pretending they were secretly watching pirates gallivant about the main deck from just below the gunwale.

Inside, he saw Leonard gesticulating his arms wildly, but not facing the window. Sam set his jaw and flared his nostrils, angry at the sight of the thin man. He could see his mother's back and shoulders. She partially obscured the rest of the room by the way she stood.

Where was Amelia?

With the communist's back turned, Sam allowed himself a few more inches of viewing space. Sweet relief washed over him. There she was, looking a little scared, but no worse for wear. Even when facing down a crazed gunman, she looked stunning.

Sam began to run scenarios in his mind. Leonard was moving erratically inside the house. He didn't want to risk taking a shot at him through the window. He could miss, or even hit Amelia, who was too closely aligned with the man to allow for a safe shot. Even if he hit Leonard, unless it was a kill shot, he would no doubt take the opportunity to bring someone with him into the afterlife. That was unacceptable. Sam began to look around for another option.

The tree!

Elijah used to climb up and down the great oak when he felt like entering or exiting his bedroom unnoticed. Sam was no slouch when it came to climbing, either. The problem was that the tree was clearly visible from the front window, and unless he grew cat claws, the only way he could make it up was by exposing his back to the house and using the knots and old stubs of limbs adorning that side.

He would need a distraction.

Leonard's back remained turned on Sam. Raising his head still higher in the window frame, Sam searched out Amelia's attention. He could see her eyes widen with surprise and beam with joy. She'd seen him. Amelia quickly made her face a blank slate, not wanting to tip Leonard off that the cavalry, finally, had come. Sam pointed to the tree. Amelia's eyes drifted in its direction and then back to Sam, pausing at a point in Leonard's raving where he focused his attention on her. He had mainly been shouting at Alice.

Amelia blinked evenly at Sam, letting him know she understood. He pantomimed climbing, pointed at Leonard, and put his hands over his eyes like a blindfold. Amelia blinked again, giving no other impression that she was communicating with someone outside of the home.

Sam took a deep breath, ready to make his move. Amelia was still looking at him. Sam wavered, locked onto her eyes, and mouthed silent words to her. The faintest fraction of a smile crossed her red lips and she blinked again, longer this time.

Squatting down to keep as far below the windows as possible, Sam moved across the front lawn and began to climb the old oak tree, feeling unbearable tension until finally climbing out of view from the front picture window. He expected to be shot in the back at any moment, and let out his breath after climbing as high as the roof-line.

A great limb served as a sort of balance beam to Sam as he traversed toward the roof, arms extended out like a tight-rope walker. The branch was a few feet taller than a flat section of roofing outside his brother's old bedroom window. He would have to jump, and hope that his landing wasn't loud enough to be heard two stories below. He didn't want a screaming madman with a gun waiting for him.

With a breath, Sam leapt from the limb, feeling his foot slip as he did so. His leather shoes weren't ideal for climbing. The loss of traction caused him to fall short, and he had to collapse his knees and hug his stomach against the shingles to keep from falling into the flowerbed below. That would have spoiled any chance of surprise. His mother's rhododendrons, too.

Pulling himself up by his fingertips, he grimaced at the heat radiating off the asphalt shingles, victims of the July sun. It was like lying across the hood of his father's Cadillac after a drive to Seaside. He moved to the bedroom window, the soles of his shoes scraping as he went.

The window was closed. He tried to lift it open, but it was either stuck or locked. Either way, he wouldn't be able to get in short of breaking the glass, and he was sure that would be heard downstairs.

Sam moved carefully towards his mother's bedroom window, as much to keep from falling as to stay quiet. He breathed a sigh of relief. The window was open, ready to take in any breezes heaven might send to provide relief. Sam went in head first, lowering himself down from a sort of elevated push-up position, hands and then long legs crawling through the window like a well-dressed spider.

Standing in the room, Sam listened for signs of being discovered. Leonard's raving demands that someone show him where to find the atomic secrets wafted upstairs. Sam nodded in thanks. Sweat had emerged from every pore in his body. He wiped his head with the sleeve of his jacket and then removed the outer layer, thankful for the instant cool that followed.

Pulling his gun, Sam held the weapon in both hands and silently stalked toward the staircase. He was grateful that there hadn't been another gunshot, and he wondered who that first shot was for. Maybe only a warning to let them know he was deadly serious.

A warm wind blew at Sam's back. He froze; the warmth seemed to be passing through his body. Sam turned and nearly shouted, giving the game up. "Dad?"

Frank held a finger to his lips, requesting silence. "I knew you'd come, Son. Don't storm the castle yet. I've arranged for a helpful diversion. Get as close as you can, but don't let him see you. He's a killer, Samuel."

Sam nodded and began making his way down the stairs. He knew every squeaky floorboard in the house, and which stairs to skip when wanting to make a silent descent. He stopped midway down. He would have to jump past three steps to avoid making any noise. That was possible going up, but not on the way down, even for his long legs. The conversation below seemed to have died down, making his need for silence all the more paramount.

Coiled like a spring, Sam waited tensely, his father next to him. A trio of frightened voices sounded from below—Alice, Amelia, and what must have been Leonard. The diversion arrived. Sam bounded down the stairs.

A gun fired and glass shattered. Sam's heart nearly stopped. The screaming renewed, this time with a fourth voice added to the mix. A voice that was distinctively southern.

Amelia listened patiently as Leonard's seemingly inexhaustible list of insults, profanity, innuendo, and curses pelted her like hail stones. She was dying to shut the filthy little man up. What was taking Sam so long?

"I swear," Leonard said, beginning to lose both breath and steam, "I swear on Lenin's tomb, that if one of you don't tell me how to find those files, or whatever they are, I'll—" He inclined his ear toward the picture window. "Does anyone else hear that?"

CLIPPITY-CLOP. CLIPPITY-CLOP.

"Like hoof beats."

The sound grew nearer. A horse in a full run.

Dropping the gun to his side, Leonard turned to the window. A black charger, foaming at the mouth, leapt through the window ghost-like, landing at a standstill right in the middle of the living room. Seated on the horse's back was a man dressed in the riding fineries of a Confederate era soldier. He held the reigns with one gloved hand. Tassels twirled and his drawn saber flashed as he whirled the sword in circles overhead.

Amelia and Alice screamed in fright at the apparition's appearance. Leonard screamed as well, without realizing he was doing so. He raised his pistol and fired straight into the soldier's chest. The bullet passed through the specter harmlessly, shattering the front picture window. The women screamed again at the shot. Leonard paused for breath and took to yelling again. Like a klaxon he screamed on, lowering his ineffective weapon in horror.

Captain Jeremiah Buford pointed his sword directly at the thin man. Unleashing a rebel yell, he spurred his steed onward and directly at Leonard, making a ghostly slash at his neck as he passed. The horse and rider carried on through the house, exiting through the wall.

Sam burst down the stairs, his father's pistol in hand, Frank right on his heels. He pointed the gun at Leonard, who was huddled into a cowering ball from the charge.

"Drop the gun and stand up slowly," Sam said.

The thin man did as he was told, the gun thudding on the floor. He stood slowly, the spectral nature of his attacker dawning on him. With hands up in surrender, a smug grin came to his face. "You already blew it with the police. Who's going to believe you, Rockwell?"

Leonard didn't even flinch as the business end of a brass lamp swung into his face. He never saw it coming. The attack hit home, re-breaking his nose. The thin man fell to the ground like a pile of sticks. Amelia set the lamp down and dusted off her hands. "I've wanted to do that for two days."

Sam smiled at her, his perspiration making Dimitry's dried blood come alive again as it rolled off his face.

"You're hurt," Alice said from across the room.

Sam holstered his weapon. "This time the blood isn't mine." He turned to Amelia. "Did I ever tell you how much I love you?"

Amelia smiled. "You might have, earlier. But I couldn't quite hear through the window. Why don't you tell me again?"

Before Sam could answer, a shower of broken glass crashed into the room from what remained of the front window. Alice shrieked as the big Russian rolled in, blood dried and matted against his skin, with fresh flows coming from the shards of glass embedded in his rocky shoulders and arms.

With all the swiftness of a tiger pouncing on its prey, Dimitry was on Sam, death still blazing in his eyes, arms again reaching for a throat to crush. "Kill you, Rockwell," was all he said, repeating it like an insane mantra.

"Kill you, Rockwell. Kill you, Rockwell." The powerful arms again overpowered Sam, and the Russian's great hands closed around his throat.

"Kill. You. Rockwell."

Amelia hurled herself onto the broad back of the Russian, scratching and clawing at his face and eyes. Keeping one hand firmly wrapped around Sam's throat, Dimitry reached behind his head, grabbed hold of Amelia, and threw her across the room, knocking over a sitting chair in the process.

"Him first," Dimitry said to Amelia, his trance broken. "You, next."

Sam struggled underneath his grip, trying desperately to escape. Somehow he doubted that Eamon would show up again to intervene. It didn't matter. He would overcome the Russian. He would not die in front of everyone he loved.

Alice was frozen in fear and disbelief. Frank had gone to her side during the earlier commotion. He watched as Amelia struggled to her feet and again moved to attack Dimitry.

"No. Stay back," Frank shouted to Amelia. "You'll get hurt." He looked to his son, struggling for life on the floor. "Alice, run and get a knife from the kitchen. Fight for her, Samuel! You fight for her!"

Sam disengaged his right hand from holding back the strangulation, the fight a mirror image of the row hours prior. The pain intensified and he felt as if his eyes were going to explode from their sockets. Dimitry locked his arms to increase the pressure on Sam's throat, leaving a gap between the two men's chests. Sam reached across his body for his pistol.

Dimitry's murderous face showed a sudden shock from the two bullets Sam fired into his chest. The rage faded, and the eyes dimmed. The Russian slumped, dead, on top of Sam.

Gasping for air, thankful for life, Sam smiled as Amelia threw her arms around him, weeping tears of joy.

CHAPTER FIFTEEN

Detective Clemons watched as two officers led Leonard away in cuffs. He surveyed the blood and broken glass littering the Rockwell's home. He was glad that he'd followed the feeling in his gut when his secretary delivered Sam's message. He really had sworn off ever seeing the man again. "That was some quick thinking inside by everyone. Things could have turned out much worse. I'm sorry I didn't believe you, Sam."

"Don't mention it," Sam said hoarsely. "So I'm okay to work as Return Detective again?"

"Fine by me."

"I'm sorry, too," Frank said to the group. "I let my fears about parting with Alice get the better of me. I lost all my discipline and it nearly cost me my wife and son. Oh, and you too, Amelia."

Clemons looked down, then back up at Frank. His gaze meandered to the mustachioed man dressed as a confederate soldier marveling at all the wonders contained in Alice's kitchen. "Those two were bad news. If you hadn't flushed them out who knows what other sort of damage they might have caused. We're lucky it wasn't worse. Well, I've got a lot of work to do." The detective clapped Sam on the shoulder as he passed. "You saved my career, Rockwell. Thanks again."

"Well, that all wrapped up rather nicely," said a decidedly British voice from behind the group. They turned to see Eamon, hands clasped together in front of him. "Are we ready to go?" he called to Frank and Captain Buford.

"So soon?" said Alice. "Can't we at least find out about that letter and the haunted horseman that jumped through my living room window?"

Eamon leaned in close to Frank, "Be quick about it."

"Well," Frank said, "the letter was a gag one of my bowling pals gave me. A forgery. The key, as I'm sure you know dear, unlocks my liquor cabinet."

"Elijah would've loved to know where that was," Sam said.

Alice looked at Captain Buford, who patted the spectral nose of his horse in the kitchen. She turned to Frank and asked, "How on earth did you arrange for a rebel soldier to ride his horse into our living room?"

"I believe I can provide that answer, ma'am," came the Dixie voice of Captain Buford. "Frank here recognized a slight resemblance between Leonard Buford and myself. The scoundrel, sad to say, is my distant kin. Frank went back and called for the clerks to look into my Returning to help. Because of my relation, the request was granted."

"And now," Eamon said, "it's time for you both to move on. Last goodbyes for a while Frank. I'll give you a bit of privacy." Eamon, Buford, and his steed, disappeared.

Frank held out his hand to Alice. Hesitating, she reached out her own hand and held it to his, her fingertips passing gently through him. "Your hand," she said, "it's warm."

"I've changed, Ally."

Alice wiped away tears. "I love you, Frank."

"I love you, too," Frank said, warmly embracing his wife the best any spook could. He turned to Sam, "Don't wait on the things that really matter. You can travel, make money, acquire power anytime you want to. But you'll only have so many years with the ones you love." Frank nodded to Amelia and returned his gaze to Sam, warming his shoulder with his ghostly touch. "Trust me son, those years can't start soon enough."

As if on cue, Eamon reappeared. "That was some excellent work tonight Samuel," he said. "Tonight when you fall asleep and dream of your father, make sure and sign for your license, all right? We could use a man like you, always willing to help."

"Thanks, I will."

Frank whispered into his son's ear. "In case you ever do need them, the real plans are hidden behind a false wall in my office safe."

Sam stared at his father in disbelief.

"Alice," Frank said, "Why not let Samuel have the Cadillac? I think he's earned it." Frank winked and, together with Eamon, disappeared. Sam, Amelia, and Alice knew they would see him again, but the lumps in their throats and tears in their eyes came, all the same.

"I think I'd better start picking up this mess," Alice said, her voice quivering. "Nothing like a good cleaning to help clear your mind."

She walked back into the house.

Sam held Amelia tightly, looking on at the pink and golden sunset burning against the snowy white of Mount Rainier.

"Oh, thank heavens," a voice called from down the street. "I was worried I wouldn't get back in time to warn you. I'm glad you're both all right." Reverend Barnaby frowned slightly. "Everything is all right?"

Amelia looked up to Sam, holding his hand as he gripped her shoulder.

"It all worked out," Sam said. "But stay in town for a while, okay Reverend? We might need you." He looked down to Amelia and pulled her close. "I'm going to take Amelia to the mountain tomorrow. There's something I want to ask her."

'TIL DEATH

ACKNOWLEDGEMENTS

This is my first novel. Going into it, I heard repeatedly from other authors in books, blogs, forums, and podcasts that it would be a lot of hard work—they weren't kidding! And so, it's with a tremendous sense of gratitude that I acknowledge all the wonderful spots of grace God provided in making this book a reality.

My wife Jenn (who I love so much!) put her English degree in my service as an Alpha Reader. I'm so thankful for the patient encouragement that accompanied all my writing sessions. Not to mention her Sauron-like eye when it came to catching typos.

Two authors helped me on this journey more than they know; Michael Bunker & Nick Cole. Michael was a tremendous guide in leading me to Independent Publishing. His book Brother, Frankenstein is a prime example of the sort of quality that's out there. Nick is an amazing writer and mentor, the Obi-Wan to my... Anakin? I'm glad to call him a friend. Check out his book The Old Man and the Wasteland. I'm blessed to be shown the ropes by the best.

Veteran authors and Beta Readers were a big help in providing guidance and keeping me grounded. Thanks to David Bruns, Kim Wells, Chris Pourteau, Hank Garner, Arthur Sido, & Amy Jo Hicks.

My father, Robert Anspach, provided invaluable insight as a former Private Investigator and Cold War counterintelligence operative.

Thanks to my sons Caleb & Owen. When they jumped up and down in excitement as I read them the fight scenes, I knew I was on to something.

M.S. Corley designed the excellent cover and patiently helped me through the process. Having a Corley cover is a feather in any indie author's hat.

Lastly: Thanks Mom. Growing up, you introduced me to the wonderful motion pictures of the 1940s and 50s that inspired so much of this book. I think fondly of all the times you started my day by throwing open my bedroom curtains while cheerfully singing "Good Morning" like Debbie Reynolds in Singin' in the Rain. Every child should be so blessed.

A Note to my Readers

I appreciate you immensely, dear reader. As an avid reader myself, I'm humbled and honored that you spent your time reading my story. I hope you enjoyed 'til Death and found it time well spent.

May I ask for one more favor? Please consider taking the time to review this book at amazon.com, and also at goodreads, if you're a member. I love hearing from my readers and your feedback will also help other readers like yourself make a sound decision about whether to spend their money, or time, on a book.

Leaving an honest review is one of the most helpful things you can do for an author—it makes a big difference in the world of independent publishing.

ABOUT THE AUTHOR

Jason Anspach lives in the Pacific Northwest with his wife and their six children. Swing by **www.JasonAnspach.com** to say hello, or email him at Jason@JasonAnspach.com.

Facebook: facebook.com/authorjasonanspach
Twitter: @Jonspach

- My newsletter pals receive updates, free books, exclusive sneak-peaks and more! Sign up today: bit.ly/anspach-news

Fans of comedy and the more traditional style of fantasy should check out the podcast, Sci-Fi Writers Playing Old School D&D at the website **www.oldschooldnd.com** — Jason writes and plays the Barbarian, which isn't much of a stretch.

Made in the USA
Charleston, SC
15 August 2015